लालू-लीला

लालू-लीला

सुशील कुमार मोदी

प्रभात प्रकाशन, दिल्ली
ISO 9001:2015 प्रकाशक

प्रकाशक • **प्रभात प्रकाशन**
4/19 आसफ अली रोड,
नई दिल्ली-110002

संस्करण • प्रथम, 2019

LALU-LEELA *by* Shri Sushil Kumar Modi
Published by Prabhat Prakashan, 4/19 Asaf Ali Road, New Delhi-2
e-mail: prabhatbooks@gmail.com ISBN 978-93-5322-073-0

लालू परिवार के भ्रष्टाचार का जीवंत दस्तावेज

श्री सुशील कुमार मोदी की सद्यः प्रकाशित पुस्तक '**लालू लीला**' लालू परिवार के भ्रष्टाचार की अंतहीन दास्तानों का जीवंत दस्तावेज है। यह भ्रष्टाचार के खिलाफ श्री मोदी के अनथक संघर्ष का ही परिणाम है कि 27 जुलाई, 2017 को बिहार में दूसरी बार सत्ता-परिवर्तन संभव हो पाया। मुझे खुशी है कि उन्होंने श्री लालू प्रसाद व उनके परिवार द्वारा किए गए भ्रष्टाचार के मुद्दे पर लगातार 40 से ज्यादा प्रेस कॉन्फ्रेंस कर मामलों को उजागर किया, जो एक रिकॉर्ड है।

श्री लालू प्रसाद के बहुचर्चित चारा घोटाला को वर्ष 1996 में उजागर करने में सुशीलजी की महत्त्वपूर्ण भूमिका रही है। उस मामले में वे याचिकाकर्ता थे और मैं उनका वकील था। इस घोटाले के विभिन्न मामलों में लालूजी के खिलाफ पर्याप्त और प्रामाणिक साक्ष्य होने के कारण न केवल उन्हें मुख्यमंत्री की कुर्सी गँवानी पड़ी बल्कि उन्हें व उनके मंत्रिमंडल के लगभग आधा दर्जन मंत्रियों को जेल भी जाना पड़ा था। फिलहाल वे इस घोटाले के चार मामलों में सजायाफ्ता हैं। उस समय सुशीलजी ने बिहार में हुए अलकतरा घोटाला को भी उजागर किया, जिसमें विभागीय मंत्री तक को जेल जाना पड़ा।

उस दौर में लालू प्रसाद का पराभव काफी मुश्किल प्रतीत होता था, परंतु चारा घोटाला, अलकतरा घोटाला आदि के उजागर होने पर कुछ ही वर्षों में बिहार का माहौल बदला और वर्ष 2005 में सत्ता-परिवर्तन संभव हो सका।

श्री लालू प्रसाद आदतन भ्रष्टाचारी हैं। चारा घोटाले से सबक लेने के बजाय अपने रेलमंत्रित्व काल में उन्होंने 'रेलवे टेंडर' घोटाला किया। श्री शिवानंद तिवारी, श्री ललन सिंह और श्री शरद यादव को वर्ष 2008 में ही इसकी भनक लग चुकी थी। उन्होंने तत्कालीन प्रधानमंत्री डॉ. मनमोहन सिंह

को ज्ञापन देकर इसकी जाँच की माँग भी की थी, किंतु यू.पी.ए. सरकार श्री लालू प्रसाद को बचाने में लगी रही।

सुशीलजी ने एक बार फिर लालू प्रसाद व उनके परिवार द्वारा भ्रष्टाचार से अर्जित अकूत बेनामी संपत्ति को पर्याप्त प्रमाण व दस्तावेजों के साथ सिलसिलेवार ढंग से उजागर किया है। इसके परिणामस्वरूप इन मामलों में जहाँ सी.बी.आई. ने चार्जशीट दाखिल कर दी है, वहीं ई.डी. ने भी लालू परिवार के 29 भूखंडों को जब्त कर लिया है।

इन मामलों में मुकदमा दर्ज होने के बाद मुख्यमंत्री श्री नीतीश कुमार ने श्री लालू प्रसाद के पुत्र व तत्कालीन उपमुख्यमंत्री श्री तेजस्वी प्रसाद यादव को अपना पक्ष रखने का अवसर दिया, लेकिन वे अपने ऊपर लगे आरोपों में से किसी एक का भी स्पष्टीकरण नहीं दे पाए।

अंततः 26 जुलाई, 2017 को श्री नीतीश कुमार ने मुख्यमंत्री पद से इस्तीफा देकर महागठबंधन से नाता तोड़ लिया और बिहार में एन.डी.ए. की सरकार बनी। यह दूसरा अवसर था, जब लालू प्रसाद के भ्रष्टाचार के कारण बिहार में सत्ता-परिवर्तन हुआ और निश्चित रूप से इसका श्रेय सुशीलजी को जाता है।

जे.पी. आंदोलन के प्रखर सेनानी श्री सुशील कुमार मोदी भ्रष्टाचार के खिलाफ संघर्ष व जीवटता के प्रतीक हैं। अखिल भारतीय विद्यार्थी परिषद् और जे.पी. आंदोलन में हम दोनों ने लंबे समय तक कार्य किया है। आज भी राजनीतिक यात्रा में सहयात्री हैं। भ्रष्टाचार के विरुद्ध लड़ना उनका सदैव संकल्प रहा है। उनकी पुस्तक 'लालू लीला' की सफलता की कामना करते हुए मैं उन्हें सामाजिक दायित्वों का निर्भीकतापूर्वक निर्वहन करने के लिए हार्दिक बधाई देता हूँ।

—रवि शंकर प्रसाद

केंद्रीय मंत्री, कानून व न्याय, इलेक्टॉनिक्स एवं आई.टी.,
भारत सरकार

संपत्ति बटोरने की लीला निराली···

अपने शुरुआती दिनों में अक्सर लालू प्रसाद यह दावा करते थे कि उनका जन्म अत्यंत गरीब परिवार में हुआ है। अपने माँ-बाप व चपरासी भाई की गरीबी का बखान कर लोगों की तालियाँ बटोरते थे। मगर सत्ता में आने के चंद वर्षों में गरीबों के गरीहा बननेवाले लालू प्रसाद अकूत संपत्ति के मालिक बन गए। चारा घोटाले के चार मामलों में सजायफ्ता लालू प्रसाद के लिए राजनीति और सत्ता संपत्ति अर्जित करने का जरिया बन गई।

लालू परिवार की भ्रष्टाचार जनित अकूत बेनामी संपत्ति की पड़ताल आसान नहीं था। शुरुआती दौर में मिट्टी घोटाला सामने आया। इसी मिट्टी घोटाले की कोख से रेलवे टेंडर घोटाले के जरिए पटना की बेशकीमती साढ़े तीन एकड़ जमीन पर बन रहे बिहार के सबसे बड़े मॉल का पर्दाफाश हुआ। मॉल की तहकीकात से खोखा कंपनियाँ उजागर होती चली गईं। इसी क्रम में दान, वसीयत, लीज व पावर ऑफ एटॉर्नी द्वारा संपत्ति हथियाने की परत-दर-परत दास्ताँ सामने आई।

लालू प्रसाद ने विधायक, पार्षद, सांसद और मंत्री बनाने के एवज में जहाँ रघुनाथ झा, कांति सिंह जैसे अनेक नेताओं से जमीन-मकान दान में लिखवा लिया, वहीं भ्रष्टाचार से कमाए कालेधन को सफेद करने के लिए बीपीएल श्रेणी के ललन चौधरी, रेलवे के खलासी हृदयानंद चौधरी तथा भूमिहीन प्रभुनाथ यादव, चंद्रकांता देवी, सुभाष चौधरी तक से नौकरी, ठेका या अन्य लाभ पहुँचाने के एवज में कीमती जमीन-मकान दान के जरिए हासिल कर लिया।

लालू परिवार ने अपने रिश्तेदारों को भी बेनामी संपत्ति हासिल करने का माध्यम बनाया। भाई के समधियाने, अपने ससुराल, बेटी के ससुराल के रिश्तेदारों के नाम से पहले अपने कालेधन से जमीन-मकान खरीदा और बाद में पत्नी, बेटों व बेटियों के नाम गिफ्ट करवा लिया। ऐसे करीब एक दर्जन मामले उजागर हुए हैं, जिनमें लालू परिवार ने करोड़ों की संपत्ति कौड़ियों के दाम पर राजनेताओं, अपने कारिंदों या रिश्तेदारों से दान करवा लिया।

लालू परिवार ने दान (Gift) के अलावा वसीयत एवं पावर ऑफ एटॉर्नी के द्वारा भी संपत्ति लिखवाने का नया फार्मूला इजाद किया। साधारणतया जब किसी संपत्ति का मालिक अन्य दूरस्थ शहर में रहता है तथा स्वयं संपत्ति की देखभाल, किराए पर लगाने या बिक्री करने के लिए समय नहीं निकाल पाता है तो वह किसी विश्वस्त को पावर ऑफ अटार्नी (Power Of Attorny) द्वारा यह कानूनी अधिकार स्थानांतरित कर देता है।

कुमार राकेश रंजन तथा मो. शमीम को विधान पार्षद बनाने की एवज में कुमार राकेश रंजन तथा उनकी पत्नी सीमा वर्मा एवं मो. शमीम तथा उनकी पत्नी सोफिया तब्बसुम की पटना शहर की करोड़ों की जमीन के मालिक पावर ऑफ एटॉर्नी के माध्यम से बन बैठे। गोपालगंज के सुभाष चंद्र चौधरी की 2 कट्ठा जमीन भी पावर ऑफ एटॉर्नी के जरिए ही हासिल कर लिया।

पावर ऑफ एटॉर्नी की अवधि व्यक्ति के जीवन काल तक ही मान्य है। अत: पावर ऑफ एटॉर्नी देनेवाले राकेश रंजन, सीमा वर्मा, मो. शमीम और सोफिया तब्बसुम से राबड़ी देवी ने अपने बेटों तेजस्वी एवं तेज प्रताप के नाम उन जमीनों का वसीयत भी करवा लिया। यानी राकेश रंजन एवं मो. शमीम एवं उनकी पत्नियों के जीवन पर्यंत राबड़ी देवी जमीन की मालिक बनी रहेंगी तथा पावर ऑफ एटॉर्नी देनेवालों की मृत्यु के बाद वसीयत के आधार पर तेजस्वी और तेज प्रताप जमीन के मालिक बन जाएँगे।

लालू प्रसाद ने संपत्ति हथियाने में आधा दर्जन से ज्यादा मुखौटा कंपनियों (Shell Company) का इस्तेमाल करने में राबर्ट वाड्रा को भी मात कर दिया। इन सभी शेल कंपनियों के माध्यम से संपत्ति हथियाने का एक ही तरीका

था—किसी बंद पड़ी कंपनी में काला धन लगाकर कंपनी के नाम जमीन/संपति खरीदना, फिर उस कंपनी के पुराने डायरेक्टर को हटाकर परिवार के लोगों को डायरेक्टर नियुक्त करना, कौड़ी के भाव सभी शेयर खरीद लेना और अंततः पूरी जमीन/संपति सहित कंपनी का मालिक बन जाना। इसी तकनीक का प्रयोग कर डिलाइट मार्केटिंग को साढ़े तीन एकड़ जमीन के मालिक बन गए, जिस पर तेजस्वी का 750 करोड़ का 'Biggest Mall Of Bihar' बन रहा था। फेयर ग्रो प्रा.लि. के माध्यम से टाटा स्टील के पटना स्थित गेस्ट हाउस के मालिक बन गए। ए.के. इंफोसिस्टम्स, केएचके होल्डिंग, मिशेल पैकर्स जैसी मुखौटा कंपनियों पर कब्जा कर तेजस्वी, राबड़ी, मीसा भारती, चंदा यादव पटना एवं दिल्ली के करोड़ों की संपत्ति के मालिक बन बैठे।

श्री अनवर अहमद को विधान पार्षद बनाने की एवज में उसके आवामी को-ऑपरेटिव बैंक, पटना से समय-समय पर ऋण प्राप्त करने एवं नोटबंदी के बाद मजदूरों के नाम पर फर्जी खाते खोलकर 500 एवं 1000 के करोड़ों के नोट जमा करवा लिए गए। सीबीआई ने अनवर के बेटे एवं अन्य को गिरफ्तार किया है और पूरे मामले की जाँच कर रही है।

आखिर लालू परिवार इतने कम समय में 141 भूखंड के अतिरिक्त 30 फ्लैट एवं आधे दर्जन मकानों के मालिक कैसे बन गए? चपरासी क्वार्टर से शुरू हुई लालू प्रसाद की यात्रा की परिणति हजार करोड़ से ज्यादा के चारा घोटाले से जुड़े 4 मामलों में सजा के रूप में हुई। मात्र 29 साल की उम्र में तेजस्वी यादव 52 से ज्यादा संपत्ति के मालिक कैसे बन गए? पुश्तैनी कोई संपत्ति नहीं थी। इंटर की पढ़ाई भी नहीं कर पाए। क्रिकेट में भी विफल रहे। आखिर ऐसी क्या योग्यता थी, जिसके बलबूते 52 संपत्ति के मालिक बन गए? तेज प्रताप 28 संपत्ति के और मीसा भारती 23 से ज्यादा संपत्ति की मालकिन हैं।

राबड़ी देवी पटना शहर में 43 भूखंड के अलावा 30 से ज्यादा फ्लैटों की भी मालकिन हैं। इन्ही में से 8 फ्लैट एक ही दिन बालू माफिया सुभाष यादव एवं राजद के संदेश से विधायक अरुण यादव को 4 करोड़ 28 लाख

में बेचा हुआ दिखाया गया है।

साइकिल पर चलनेवाले लालू प्रसाद आज 40 लाख की मर्सिडिज बेंज कार एवं बेटा तेज प्रताप 20 लाख की हार्ले डेविडसन मोटरसाइकिल एवं 30 लाख की बीएमडब्ल्यू कार के मालिक हैं।

श्रीमती राबड़ी देवी ने 75 लाख श्रेया कंस्ट्रक्शन, 26 लाख तेज प्रताप, 1 करोड़ राहुल यादव एवं 50 लाख किसी सुबोध कुमार से कर्ज ले रखा है। श्री लालू प्रसाद ने बालू माफिया सुभाष प्रसाद यादव से 25 लाख एवं राज्य सभा सांसद प्रेमचंद गुप्ता से 15 लाख का कर्ज ले रखा है। राबड़ी देवी ने राम किशुन सिंह से 48 लाख, बबिता कुमारी से 51 लाख एवं श्रेया कंस्ट्रक्शन से 50 लाख अग्रिम ले रखा है।

पत्नी, बेटों, बेटियों के लिए ही नहीं आनेवाली तीन-तीन पीढ़ियों के लिए संपत्ति बटोरने की हवस का नाम लालू प्रसाद है। वाकई लालू प्रसाद की संपत्ति हासिल करने की लीला निराली है।

—सुशील कुमार मोदी

अनुक्रम

प्राक्कथन : लालू परिवार के भ्रष्टाचार का जीवंत दस्तावेज — *5*

लेखकीय : संपत्ति बटोरने की लीला निराली¨ — *7*

लालू परिवार के भ्रष्टाचार की अंतहीन दास्ताँ — **17**

खोखा कंपनियों के जरिए अकूत बेनामी संपत्ति

डिलाइट मार्केटिंग प्रा. लि. — 19

- कोचर की इसी 3.5 एकड़ जमीन पर बन रहा है 750 करोड़ का बिहार का सबसे बड़ा मॉल — 20
- बिना पर्यावरण की अनुमति के मॉल के निर्माण पर केंद्र की रोक — 21
- बिना नक्शा पास कराए हो रहा था मॉल का निर्माण — 23
- साजिश, धोखाधड़ी एवं आपराधिक कृत्य के खिलाफ सी.बी.आई. ने दर्ज की एफ.आई.आर. और चार्जशीट — 25
- मिट्टी घोटाला : मुफ्त के आम, गुठलियों के दाम — 50

ए.के. इन्फोसिस्टम्स प्रा.लि. — **53**

हर काम के लिए जमीन

फेयर ग्रो होल्डिंग्स प्रा.लि. — **56**

टाटा स्टील के दो मंजिला मकान के मालिक बन गए तेजस्वी

- टिस्को की संपत्ति तेजस्वी को देने के लिए सहारा समूह ने भुगतान किया — 61
- टाटा एवं सहारा समूह को उपकृत करने के एवज में ली गई संपत्ति — 62

ए.बी. एक्सपोर्ट्स प्रा.लि. 64
रंग चोखा करने का नायाब नुस्खा

मिशेल पैकर्स एंड प्रिंटर्स प्रा.लि. 67
काले धन को ठिकाने लगाने का जरिया

के.एच.के. होल्डिंग प्रा.लि. 70
मनी लाउंड्रिंग का खेल

दान के मुखौटे से जमीन/मकान हथियाने का गोरखधंधा 73

कांति सिंह ने मंत्री बनने के लिए
अपनी संपत्ति लीज पर दी और दान की 74

कांति सिंह ने तेजस्वी–तेज प्रताप को जमीन–मकान किया गिफ्ट 77

रघुनाथ झा ने मंत्री पद की चाहत में
करोड़ों की संपत्ति को कर दिया दान 80

ललन चौधरी : लालू के 'भामाशाह' 82

हृदयानंद चौधरी : रेलवे के खलासी की दानवीरता 86

प्रभुनाथ यादव : रिश्ते का सौदा। 89

सुभाष चौधरी : लालू के पैसों से
जमीन खरीद मीसा को किया दान 91

चंद्रकांता चौधरी : सास–बहू का दान का रिश्ता 92

रमा देवी से तेज प्रताप को 3 वर्ष 8 माह की उम्र में
13 एकड़ 12 डिसमिल जमीन मिली दान में 93

गिफ्ट कैंसिल कराने का दावा 95

मंगरू यादव को भी नहीं बख्शा 98
लालू लोगों से बख्शीश लेते रहे
परंतु कभी किसी को बख्शीश नहीं दी

तीन पीढ़ियों का इंतजाम 100
एम.एल.सी. बनाने के एवज में 4 प्लॉट का राबड़ी देवी के
नाम पॉवर ऑफ एटॉर्नी और तेजस्वी-तेज प्रताप के नाम वसीयत

सुभाष चंद्र चौधरी ने भी पावर ऑफ एटॉर्नी के माध्यम से
राबड़ी को सौंप दी जमीन 104

लीज द्वारा 255 डिसमिल जमीन के
मालिक बने तेजस्वी यादव 106

तेजस्वी केवल 750 करोड़ रुपए का मॉल
ही नहीं बनवा रहे थे, बल्कि करोड़ों के
लोहे का व्यापार भी करते हैं 109

29 साल की उम्र में तेजस्वी यादव 5 मकान,
47 जमीन सहित कुल 52 संपत्ति के मालिक 112

पेट्रोल पंप का मालिक लालू परिवार 115
तेज प्रताप का पेट्रोल पंप घोटाला

लारा इंटीरियर्स प्रा.लि.—'ला' से लालू, 'रा' से राबड़ी 118

- तेज प्रताप ने छुपाई औरंगाबाद की संपत्ति 120
- चुनाव आयोग से तेज प्रताप की
  सदस्यता रद्द करने की माँग 121
- औरंगाबाद में तेज प्रताप यादव द्वारा
  खरीदी गई जमीन का ब्योरा 124
- झूठे शपथ-पत्र के खिलाफ मुकदमा 126

बड़े भाई होने के बावजूद मात्र 26 भूखंडों एवं 2 मकान परंतु 20 लाख की मोटरसाइकिल एवं 30 लाख की BMW के मालिक तेज प्रताप 128

राजद के पूर्व मंत्री के मॉल में लालू की दूसरी बेटी रोहिणी आचार्य की संपत्ति 130

671 डिसमिल की मालकिन लालू की चौथी बेटी रागिनी 133

राबड़ी-लालू और उनके परिजनों के फ्लैट व प्लॉट 136
श्रीमती राबड़ी देवी पटना में 18 फ्लैट्स की मालकिन

लालू-बालू का रिश्ता 140
बालू माफिया ने खरीदे राबड़ी देवी के 8 फ्लैट्स

कुल 43 भूखंड एवं 30 फ्लैट की मालकिन राबड़ी देवी 143

लालू की बेटियाँ भी होड़ में शामिल 145

संपत्ति बटोरने में मीसा भारती भी पीछे नहीं 147

एम.एल.ए. को-ऑपरेटिव में पाँच प्लॉट्स का मालिक लालू परिवार 149

परिवार के लिए 141 भूखंड, 30 फ्लैट एवं 5 मकान अर्जित करनेवाले लालू मात्र 3 संपत्ति के मालिक 154

आवामी को-ऑपरेटिव बैंक लालू की दुधारू गाय 155

तेजस्वी का 750 करोड़ का मॉल बनानेवाला सुरसण्ड से राजद का विधायक अबू दोजाना Habitual offender 158

प्रवर्तन निदेशालय द्वारा जब्त संपत्ति **160**
- डिलाइट मार्केटिंग की जब्त की गई संपत्तियों का ब्योरा 160
- ए.के. इन्फोसिस्टम्स की जब्त की गई संपत्ति का ब्योरा 164
- ए.बी. एक्सपोर्ट्स की जब्त संपत्ति का ब्योरा 167
- मिशेल पैकर्स की जब्त संपत्ति का ब्योरा 167
- ललन चौधरी और हृदयानंद चौधरी की जब्त की गई संपत्ति 168

Property details
- Smt. Rabari Devi 171
- Shri Lalu Prasad Yadav 175
- Shri Tejashwi Yadav 176
- Shri Tej Pratap Yadav 178
- Miss Raj Laxmi (Daughter) 180
- Miss Dhannu (Daughter) 180
- Smt. Misha Bharti 181
- Shailesh Kumar (Spouse) 182
- Miss Durga Bharti (Dependent 1) 184
- Miss Gauri Bharti (Dependent 2) 185

लालू परिवार के मॉल, मिट्टी घोटाले एवं बेनामी संपत्ति का रिकॉर्ड 40 पी.सी. के जरिए सिलसिलेवार खुलासा **186**

लालू परिवार के भ्रष्टाचार की अंतहीन दास्ताँ

खोखा कंपनियों के जरिए अकूत बेनामी संपत्ति

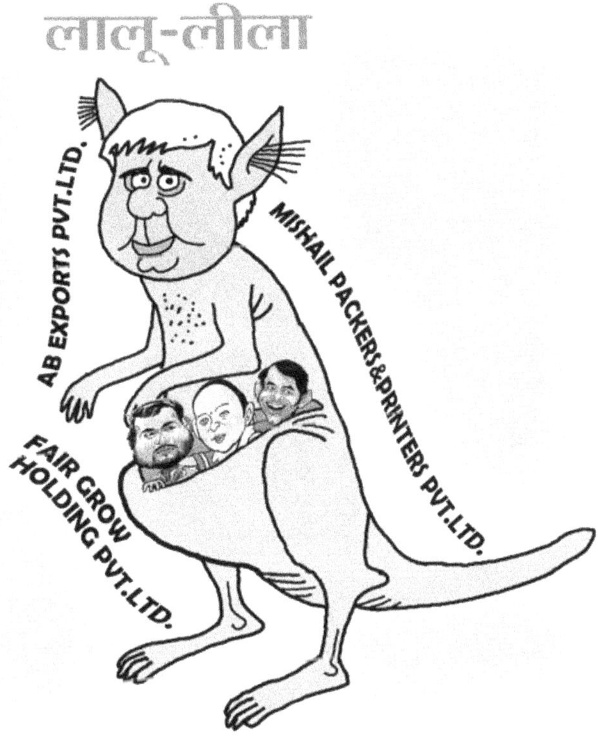

लालू प्रसाद के रेल मंत्री रहते और श्रीमती राबड़ी देवी के मुख्यमंत्रित्व काल में लालू परिवार ने अनेक मुखौटा यानी खोखा कंपनियों के जरिए न केवल करोड़ों की जमीन और मकान हथियाए बल्कि फर्जी तरीके

से शेयर खरीद और निदेशक बनकर पूरी कंपनी पर ही कब्जा कर लिया। दरअसल, किसी बंद पड़ी पुरानी कंपनी को टेक ओवर करके या नई कंपनी स्थापित कर लालू प्रसाद के रेलमंत्रित्व काल में काले धन का इस्तेमाल कर

जमीन या मकान खरीदा गया। फिर उन कंपनियों के पुराने डायरेक्टरों को हटाकर तेजस्वी, तेज प्रताप, चंदा यादव या रागिनी लालू को नया डायरेक्टर बना दिया गया। अधिकांश कंपनियों की सारी शेयर होल्डिंग लालू परिवार के सदस्यों को हस्तांतरित कर पूरी कंपनी और उसकी करोड़ों की संपत्ति पर कब्जा कर लिया गया। अब तक उजागर हुई कंपनियों में काले धन का इस्तेमाल कर बेनामी संपत्ति अपने नाम करने का कमोबेश यही तरीका अपनाया गया।

□

डिलाइट मार्केटिंग प्रा. लि.

LARA Projects Pvt. Ltd.

होटल से मॉल तक बिना ब्रेक भ्रष्टाचार की रेल

- श्री लालू प्रसाद ने मई 2004 में रेल मंत्री बनते ही सुजाता होटल्स प्रा. लि. के विनय कोचर, हर्ष कोचर, IRCTC के पदाधिकारियों तथा डिलाइट मार्केटिंग की डायरेक्टर सरला गुप्ता (पत्नी श्री प्रेमचंद गुप्ता) की मिली-भगत से रेलवे के राँची और पुरी के दो होटल हर्ष कोचर की कंपनी को 15 साल की लीज पर दे दिए।
- इन दो होटलों को लीज पर देने के एवज में हर्ष कोचर की कंपनी से 3.5 एकड़ जमीन पटना में डिलाइट मार्केटिंग के नाम 10 डीड के माध्यम से बाजार मूल्य से काफी कम कीमत पर लिखवा ली गई।
- ज्ञातव्य है कि श्री प्रेमचंद गुप्ता को श्री लालू प्रसाद ने वर्ष 2004 में कंपनी मामलों का केंद्रीय मंत्री बनवाया था। वे बाद में भी लगातार पाँच बार उन्हें राज्य सभा सांसद बनाते रहे, जबकि वे हरियाणा के रहनेवाले हैं और उनका बिहार से कभी कोई सीधा संबंध नहीं रहा।
- लालू प्रसाद अपने परिवार के नाम यदि जमीन लिखवाते तो तुरंत भंडा फूट जाता कि इन्होंने दो होटल के एवज में जमीन ले ली है, इसलिए फर्जी कंपनियों को माध्यम बनाया गया।
- श्री लालू प्रसाद ने अपने विश्वस्त सहयोगी की कंपनी डिलाइट मार्केटिंग के नाम 3.5 एकड़ जमीन लिखवा ली।
- हर्ष कोचर की कंपनी को दो होटल देने में बड़े पैमाने पर अनियमितता बरती गई और टेंडर की शर्तों को इस प्रकार बदला गया कि बिना किसी स्पर्धा के ये दोनों होटल हर्ष कोचर को दिए जा सकें।

- डिलाइट कंपनी के प्रारंभिक निदेशक ने वर्ष 2014 में इस्तीफा दे दिया और श्री तेज प्रताप, तेजस्वी यादव, श्रीमती राबड़ी देवी, चंदा यादव एवं रागिनी लालू वर्ष 2014-16 के बीच इस कंपनी के निदेशक बना दिए गए।
- वर्ष 2010-11 से डिलाइट कंपनी के शेयर्स तेजस्वी यादव और राबड़ी देवी के नाम ट्रांसफर किए जाने लगे।
- वर्ष 2014 आते-आते 85 प्रतिशत शेयर्स का स्वामित्व श्रीमती राबड़ी देवी और 15 प्रतिशत शेयर्स का स्वामित्व तेजस्वी यादव ने हासिल कर लिया।
- जिस समय तेजस्वी यादव डिलाइट कंपनी के निदेशक और शेयरधारक बने, उस समय उनकी उम्र 24 वर्ष थी।
- तेजस्वी यादव एवं राबड़ी देवी मात्र 64 लाख रुपए की पूँजी लगाकर 94 करोड़ बाजार मूल्य की संपत्ति के मालिक बन गए।
- नोटबंदी के मात्र चार दिन के भीतर तेजस्वी ने डिलाइट कंपनी का नाम बदलकर LARA (LA लालू, RA राबड़ी) Projects Pvt. Ltd. कर दिया।

कोचर की इसी 3.5 एकड़ जमीन पर बन रहा है 750 करोड़ का बिहार का सबसे बड़ा मॉल

- डिलाइट कंपनी मुख्यत: आयात निर्यात का काम करती थी; परंतु चूँकि तेजस्वी को वहाँ मॉल बनवाना था, अत: LARA कंपनी के उद्देश्य में मॉल निर्माण शामिल किया गया।
- इसी 3.5 एकड़ जमीन (मौजा—जलालपुर, दानापुर) पर तेजस्वी द्वारा बिहार के सबसे बड़ा मॉल का निर्माण कराया जा रहा था।

कोचर बंधुओं से रिश्वत में ली गई
पटना की इसी 3.5 एकड़ जमीन पर बन रहा है बिहार का सबसे बड़ा मॉल

- 1 लाख 55 हजार वर्ग फीट के इस प्लॉट पर 7 लाख 66 हजार वर्ग फीट का 'बिहार का सबसे बड़ा मॉल' बनवाया जा रहा था, जिसकी अनुमानित लागत 750 करोड़ रुपए है।
- इस मॉल का निर्माण सुरसंड के राजद विधायक श्री अबू दोजाना की कंपनी मैसर्स मेरीडियन कंस्ट्रक्शन (इंडिया) लि. द्वारा कराया जा रहा था।
- तेजस्वी का यह बिहार का सबसे बड़ा मॉल 12 मंजिला जमीन के ऊपर एवं 3 मंजिला जमीन के भीतर होगा। इसमें 1,000 दुकानें, शॉपिंग मॉल्स, मल्टीप्लेक्स, फाइव स्टार होटल एवं ऑफिस कॉम्प्लेक्स शामिल हैं।

बिना पर्यावरण की अनुमति के मॉल के निर्माण पर केंद्र की रोक

- नियमानुसार 7 लाख 66 हजार वर्ग फीट के निर्माण हेतु पर्यावरण स्वच्छता प्रमाण-पत्र की आवश्यकता थी।
- पर्यावरण संरक्षण अधिनियम, 1986 की अवहेलना कर राज्य पर्यावरण प्रभाव आकलन प्राधिकार (State Environmental Impact Assessment Authority—S.E.I.A.A.) से अनुमति प्राप्त किए बिना निर्माण प्रारंभ कर दिया गया था।

बिना नक्शा पास कराए तथा पर्यावरण क्लीयरेंस लिये किया जा रहा था मॉल का निर्माण

- मीडिया में मामला उजागर होने के बाद तेजस्वी यादव की कंपनी की ओर से निर्माण प्रारंभ होने के करीब एक साल बाद (20 अप्रैल, 2017 को) अनुमति के लिए प्राधिकार को आवेदन दिया गया।
- नियम के अनुसार, यदि अनुमति के बिना कार्य प्रारंभ कर दिया गया है तो यह अधिनियम के उल्लंघन का मामला बनता है और ऐसी स्थिति में राज्य प्राधिकार अनुमति प्रदान नहीं कर सकता; बल्कि भारत सरकार को अनुमति के लिए आवेदन देना आवश्यक होगा।

- चूँकि वन विभाग उस समय तेजस्वी प्रसाद यादव के बड़े भाई तेज प्रताप यादव के अधीन था, इस कारण वन विभाग और S.E.I.A.A. की मिली-भगत से निर्माण को रोककर प्राथगिकी दर्ज करने की कार्रवाई नहीं की गई और न ही भारत सरकार को सूचित किया गया।
- स्वयं बिल्डर दोजाना ने निर्माण शुरू होने के एक साल बाद अपने आवेदन पत्र में स्वीकार किया है कि नींव की खुदाई का काम पूरा किया जा चुका है और निर्माण प्रारंभ करने के बाद अनुमति के लिए आवेदन दिया जा रहा है।
- भारत सरकार के पर्यावरण मंत्रालय ने 15 मई, 2017 को प्रदूषण नियंत्रण बोर्ड के सदस्य सचिव, पर्यावरण विभाग के प्रधान सचिव तथा राजद विधायक अबू दोजाना को निर्देश दिया कि इस निर्माण को तत्काल रोक दिया जाए।

बिना नक्शा पास कराए हो रहा था मॉल का निर्माण

लालू प्रसाद के रेल मंत्री रहते रेलवे के दो होटल लीज पर देने के एवज में तेजस्वी को हासिल हुई 3.5 एकड़ जमीन पर बन रहे बिहार के 750 करोड़ रुपए के 15 मंजिले सबसे बड़े मॉल का निर्माण बिना नक्शा पास कराए प्रारंभ किया गया था। बिहार नगर पालिका अधिनियम, 2017 के नियम 313 में स्पष्ट प्रावधान है कि 'भवन का नक्शा स्वीकृत होने पर ही कोई व्यक्ति निर्माण करेगा।'

4 अप्रैल, 2017 को मिट्टी घोटाला उजागर होने के 11 दिन बाद आनन-फानन में आधे-अधूरे कागजात के साथ 15 अप्रैल को दानापुर नगर परिषद् में नक्शे की स्वीकृति हेतु आवेदन दिया गया। इसके लगभग सवा महीने बाद 24 मई, 2017 को नगर परिषद्, दानापुर ने नक्शे की त्रुटि के निवारण हेतु तेजस्वी यादव के वास्तुविद् को नोटिस जारी किया।

नक्शे के आवेदन में निम्न त्रुटियाँ पाई गईं—

- चेक लिस्ट अधूरी है।
- बेसमेंट का इंडेम्निटी बॉण्ड नहीं है।
- मालगुजारी रसीद अद्यतन नहीं है।
- वास्तुविद्/भू-स्वामी के मूल हस्ताक्षर नहीं हैं।
- जमीन के दस्तावेज नहीं हैं।
- अग्निशमन विभाग का अनापत्ति प्रमाण-पत्र (एन.ओ.सी.) नहीं है।
- नेशनल ग्रीन ट्रिब्यूनल का अनापत्ति प्रमाण-पत्र (एन.ओ.सी.) नहीं है।
- नक्शे की सॉफ्ट कॉपी PDF एवं CAD फॉरमैट में नहीं है।
- भू-स्थल का फोटोग्राफ नहीं है।

आज तक इन त्रुटियों का निराकरण तो दूर की बात, नोटिस का जवाब तक नहीं दिया गया है। 1 सितंबर, 2017 को कार्यपालक अधिकारी, दानापुर नगर पालिका ने जवाब अप्राप्त होने की सूचना दी और पुन: स्मारित करने का निर्णय लिया।

सवाल है कि—

- संवैधानिक पद पर बैठा व्यक्ति बिना नगर निकाय से नक्शा पारित कराए व्यावसायिक भवन का निर्माण कैसे करने की हिम्मत कर सकता है?
- मिट्टी घोटाले के बाद दिखाने के लिए एक आधा-अधूरा आवेदन दाखिल कर दिया गया।
- नोटिस मिलने के बावजूद निर्माण जारी रहा, जब तक भारत सरकार के पर्यावरण मंत्रालय ने रोक नहीं लगाई।
- अभी तक मॉल के आवश्यक कागजात दाखिल नहीं किए जा सके हैं।

साजिश, धोखाधड़ी एवं आपराधिक कृत्य के खिलाफ सी.बी.आई. ने दर्ज की एफ.आई.आर. और चार्जशीट

लालू प्रसाद के रेलमंत्रित्व काल में रेलवे के राँची और पुरी के दो होटलों को कोचर बंधुओं को लीज पर देने में की गई धोखाधड़ी, बदले में तत्कालीन कंपनी मामलों के मंत्री प्रेमचंद गुप्ता की डिलाइट मार्केटिंग कंपनी के नाम से पटना में 3.5 एकड़ जमीन लिखवाने और बाद में कंपनी सहित जमीन को लालू प्रसाद की पत्नी श्रीमती राबड़ी देवी, बेटे तेजस्वी प्रसाद यादव को देने (जिस पर बिहार का सबसे बड़ा मॉल बन रहा था) के आरोप में सी.बी.आई. ने 5 जुलाई, 2017 को आई.पी.सी. की धारा 120बी, सेक्शन 420, पी.सी. ऐक्ट 1988 की धारा 13 (2) r/w 13(1) (d) के अंतर्गत श्री लालू प्रसाद, श्रीमती राबड़ी देती, श्री तेजस्वी प्रसाद यादव, श्रीमती सरला गुप्ता—पत्नी श्री प्रेमचंद गुप्ता, श्री विजय कोचर, श्री विनय कोचर, मैसर्स लारा प्रोजेक्ट्स एल.एल.पी. और पी.के. गोयल, तत्कालीन मैनेजिंग डायरेक्टर, आई.आर.सी.टी.सी. तथा अन्य अज्ञात के खिलाफ प्राथमिकी दर्ज की तथा अगरत 2018 में चार्जशीट दाखिल कर दिया।

रेलवे होटल घोटाले में श्री लालू प्रसाद यादव व अन्य अभियुक्तों के खिलाफ सीबीआई की ओर से दाखिल चार्जशीट—

(12) Particulars of accused persons not chargesheeted: Nil

(13) (i) Particulars of witnesses relied : Attached
(ii) List of Documents : Attached

(14) If FIR is false, indicate action taken : Not applicable or proposed to be taken u/s 182 / 211 IPC

(15) Result of laboratory analysis : Not applicable

(16) Brief facts of the case.

Instant regular (criminal) case was registered by CBI on 05.07.2017 for the offences punishable u/s 120-B r/w Section 420 IPC and Section 13(2) r/w 13(1) (d) of the

P.C. Act, 1988 and substantive offences thereof against (1) Shri Lalu Prasad Yadav, the then Minister of Railways, Govt. of India; (2) Smt. Rabri Devi w/o Shri Lalu Prasad Yadav; (3) Shri Tejashwi Prasad Yadav s/o Shri Lalu Prasad Yadav; (4) M/s LARA Projects LLP (erstwhile known as M/s Lara Projects Pvt. Ltd./ M/s Delight Marketing Company Pvt. Ltd.); (5) Shri Vijay Kochhar s/o Shri Om Prakash Kochhar; (6) Shri Vinay Kochhar, s/o Shri Om Prakash Kochhar; (both Directors of M/s. Sujata Hotel Private Limited) (7) Smt. Sarla Gupta w/o Shri Prem Chand Gupta; (8) Shri P. K. Goel, the then Managing Director, IRCTC; & unknown others.

It is alleged in the FIR that Shri Lalu Prasad Yadav, while working as Minister of Railways, Govt. of India, entered into a criminal conspiracy with Kochhars of M/s Sujata Hotel Pvt. Ltd. (SHPL) (owners of Hotel Chanakya, Patna) & others, and in pursuance thereof, Shri Lalu Prasad Yadav by abusing his official position, extended undue favour to M/s SHPL, through the officers posted at IRCTC, New Delhi, in award of contract for sub-leasing of existing Railway Hotels known as BNR Hotels at Ranchi & Puri. As a consideration for this undue favour, a high value prime land at Patna was sold by Kochhar brothers to a company being run by a close aide of Shri Lalu Prasad Yadav, namely, Shri Prem Chand Gupta and his associates. Later, this company was taken over by

the family members of Shri Lalu Prasad Yaday. Thus, the said high value prime land in Patna reached the family members of Shri Lalu Prasad Yadav, at a nominal consideration.

17. Results of investigation:

The investigation conducted in this case has revealed the following:-

1. That Indian Railway Catering and Tourism Corporation Ltd. (hereinafter referred as IRCTC), is a Public

Sector Enterprise under Ministry of Railways, which was incorporated on 27th September, 1999, as an extended arm of the Indian Railways to upgrade, professionalize and manage the catering and hospitality services at stations, on trains and other locations and to promote domestic and international tourism through development of budget hotels, special tour packages, information & commercial publicity and global reservation systems.

2. That on 12.04.2001, a Memorandum of Understanding (MoU) was executed between the Ministry of Railways and IRCTC. As per Para 2.1 of the said MoU under the heading 'Transfer of land and building', it was agreed between both the parties that land and buildings owned by the Indian Railways and so identified mutually will be leased/licensed to the IRCTC ltd. on nominal licence fee/lease charges, with permission to sub- lease/sub-license the rights to third party in regard to activities related to passenger amenities and essential services like food and beverages outlets, pantry cars, passenger information services, retiring rooms/ budget hotels, pre- departure & post arrival services, development of passenger terminal etc. It was further agreed that IRCTC will not only continue to provide these essential services, but will also induce investment in their up-gradation and professionalization. It was also provided that IRCTC with the participation of private entrepreneur will manage these activities which would lead to reduction of liabilities of Indian Railways' to that extent.

3. That on 18.09.2001, Railway Board vide its letter No.2001/TG.III /600 /5, addressed to all GMs,

conveyed its decision regarding transfer of catering services including transfer of Rail Yatri Niwas and Railway Hotels to IRCTC.

4. That on 04.02.2003, Railway Board vide its letter No.2002/TG-111/600/5, addressed to all GMs and MD, IRCTC, communicated that it has been decided by the board that all catering and vending activities managed departmentally and through licencees on zonal railways, as also the management of Rail Yatri Niwas, Railway Hotels which were not been taken over by the IRCTC till then will be transferred to IRCTC on "as is where is basis".
5. That on 19.03.2004, another MoU was executed between IRCTC and the Railway Board, wherein vide its Para No.2.1, the issue regarding transfer of land & buildings was discussed and the agreement on this issue was similar to the agreement entered vide MoU dated 12.04.2001.
6. That Shri Lalu Prasad Yadav, a politician from Rashtriya Janta Dal, Party, on 22.05.2004, took charge as Minister of Railways (hereinafter referred as MR) (from 22.05.2004 to 22.05.2009), and by virtue of his position, became aware about the decision of the Railway Board to transfer operation and management of BNR hotels at Ranchi & Puri from Railways to IRCTC with a scope of participation of private entrepreneurs for sub-leasing.
7. That on 18.08.2004, the Railway Board vide its letter No.2001[TG-111/600/9, issued under the signature of Shri Kamal Kant, ED (T&C), Railway Board to GM (Catering) of all Zones & MD, IRCTC,
communicated about approval of Railway Board for transfer of management of departmental catering

services on Indian Railways including Rail Yatri Niwas at New Delhi & Howrah and Railway Hotels at Puri & Ranchi to IRCTC on "as is where is basis" with immediate effect.

8. That on 31.08.2004, Shri R.K. Singh, the then Chairman Railway Board (hereinafter referred as CRB) issued a note addressed to Member (Engineering), Member (Traffic), Financial Controller, Additional Member (Catering & Tourism), Additional Member (IT) and Additional Member (CE) for information and necessary action. A copy of the same was also marked to PS to MR for information under the heading of 'Record Note of discussion held with Hon'ble MR on telephone on 31.08.2004'. Para 1 of this note mentioned that:

   "Hon'ble MR has desired that only catering managed by private contractors pertaining to Pantry, Refreshment Room etc. should be transferred to IRCTC and departmental catering should continue to remain with the Railways at present."

   Pursuant to the aforesaid directions, the then Member Traffic recorded on file (Railway Board File No 2001/TG-III/600/9) that as per the note of Chairman Railway Board, Departmental Catering was not to be handed over to IRCTC at that time. There is no other noting of any other Railway official on this issue.

   That from the statements of concerned Railway officials who were dealing with this issue at the highest level it is revealed that BNR Hotels were a part of Departmental Catering since these were existing Railway properties and were controlled and managed by departmental staff.

9. That on 25.11.2004, the Railway Board in its meeting took up this issue and decided that for the transfer of Rail Yatri Niwas (RYN)& Railway hotels at Puri & Ranchi, the ownership will remain with Railways and transfer of property shall be on an "as is where is basis". It was also decided that revenue sharing will be governed by the MoU in addition, to payment of a nominal annual license fee of Rs.1000/-. A copy of the minutes of the said meeting was also sent to the then Minister of Railways Shri Lalu Prasad Yaday.
10. That on 25.02.2005, Railway Board vide its letter No.2004/TG- III/671/1/IRCTC, addressed to the MD, IRCTC and GM (Catering) of all zones, communicated about the lease charges for budget hotels/RYN. Vide para 3 of this letter, it was communicated that ownership of BNR hotels will remain with Indian Railways. It is relevant to mention here that on the same day i.e. 25.02.2005, 11 sale deeds were executed vide which 358 decimals of prime land at Patna was transferred by Kochhar brothers through Power of Attorney in favour of Harsh Kochhar by Vinay Kochhar, Vijay Kochhar and Arvind Kochhar to M/s Delight Marketing Company Pvt. Ltd. hereinafter referred as M/s(DMCPL) for a total consideration of Rs. 1.61 crores which was less than the prevalent circle rates.
11. That on 24.08.2005, the Railway Board in its meeting further took this issue, wherein it was decided that before considering the duration of the lease period, market should be tested and the Directorate should come up with a fresh proposal. A copy of minutes of the meeting was also sent to the then Minister of Railways Shri Lalu Prasad Yaday. However, there is

nothing on record to show whether any study to test the market to this effect was carried out.

12. That on 16.11.2005, Railway Board vide its letter No.2004/TG-111/673 /1/IRCTC issued under the signature of Dr. P.K. Goel, the

then Executive Director (T&C), Railway Board (who later became MD, IRCTC on 27.06.2006), addressed to General Managers of all Zonal Railways with a copy to Managing Director (MD), IRCTC, communicated about fixation of license fees/land lease charges for budget hotels, food plazas, RYNs and BNR hotels at Puri and Ranchi with the specific mention of the ownership of the property with Railways and maintenance to be taken over by IRCTC on 'as is where is basis'. As per this letter, lease period was to be 30 years or revised period as per board's instructions from time to time and provisions of MoU with IRCTC for the purpose.

13. That on 26.09.2006, the then CRB Shri J. P. Batra issued a note addressed to Member Traffic, who in turn marked it to Additional Member (Tourism & Catering) and MD, IRCTC wherein it has been mentioned that:

"*OSD to MR rang up and informed that MR has desired that the proposal for more budget hotels including the ones for which the advertisement has been given in papers, be withdrawn till the policy in this regard is finalized*':

The omission of BNR Hotels from the aforesaid directions is significant as the Budget Hotels along with BNR Hotels were part of a larger policy issue of Public Private Partnership for which simultaneous steps were being taken by the IRCTC officials including common advertisements dated 3.11.06 and 15.11.06.

The aforesaid facts coupled with the fact that whenever Railway Board took decisions regarding BNR Hotels, copy of Board decisions were sent to the MR, establish that Sh. Lalu Prasad Yadav, the then MR was in full knowledge of the fact that BNR Hotels were being transferred to IRCTC and the first direction issued by him on 31.08.2004 to then Chairman, Railway Board was to the effect that departmental catering should continue to remain with the Railways at that time Departmental catering included BNR Hotels at Ranchi and Puri as they were part of existing Railway properties operated and maintained by the departmental staff. It was pursuant to the conspiracy that BNR Hotels were allowed to be transferred to IRCTC.

14. That above mentioned specific directions of Shri Lalu Prasad Yadav, Minister of Railways, through abovesaid two notes of Chairman, Railway Board dated 31.08.2004 & 26.09.2006, updating about developments in the matter through minutes of Railway Board Meetings especially dated 25.11.2004 & 24.08.2005, as discussed in pre-paras, are sufficient to establish his knowledge regarding management, developments and operation of Budget Hotels and BNR hotels at Ranchi & Puri, as well as scope of participation of private parties in the matter through sub-leasing.

15. That BNR hotel Ranchi was handed over by the concerned zonal railway i.e. South Eastern Railway to IRCTC on 19.01.2006 and BNR hotel Puri was handed over by the concerned zonal railway i.e. East

Coast Railway to IRCTC on 10.02.2006.

16. That after Sh. P.K. Goel joined IRCTC as MD on 27.06.2006, a note bearing No.2006/IRCTC/RYN/General dated 10.07.2006 was initiated by Shri Rakesh Saksena, the then Director (T&M), IRCTC, wherein it was proposed to develop, maintain and operate RYN and BNR hotels through PPP in the same model as adopted for Budget Hotels with same technical specifications, reproduced therein. This note was approved by the then MD, IRCTC Shri P.K. Goel. Through this note it was also approved that the tenure of the licence be kept as 15 years.

17. That, later it was decided by the IRCTC to classify the RYN and BNR hotels according to the standard of the cities i.e. Metro City and Non-Metro City, in line which was already done for Budget Hotels and revised minimum eligibility criteria for RYN & BNR Hotels accordingly. The reason for such revision in eligibility criteria has been mentioned as to encourage reputed hotel operators to come forward for bidding at non metro stations like Ranchi & Puri but no justification for such a reasoning was given. There is also no record to justify the mooting of such proposal. For this purpose, as instructed by senior officers, a separate note having subject "Revision of Minimum Eligibility Criteria for RYN & BNR hotels" dated 06.10.2006 was initiated by Shri L. Ravi Kumar, the then Assistant Manager (Tourism), which was routed through Shri B.K. Agarwal, GGM (Tourism), Shri Rakesh Saksena, the then Director (T&M), Shri R.K. Gogia, the then JGM (Finance) and was finally approved by Shri P.K. Goel, the then MD, IRCTC on the same day. As per this classification, the eligibility criteria for BNR hotels

at Ranchi & Puri, in brief, was minimum turnover of Rs.3 crores per annum, Networth of Rs.1 crore as on 31.03.2006, positive net profit for at least 02 years of the 03 financial years i.e. 2003-04, 2004-05 & 2005-06, be in the business of operating and maintaining hotel (at least a 2-star category) for the last five financial years, not defaulted on any bank/ financial institutions in loans in the past, no statutory dues and undisputed liabilities and income tax and/ or sale tax payer.

18. That on 09.10.2006, based on the above said approval of MD, IRCTC dated 06.10.2006, an Notice Inviting Tender (NIT) was issued for RYN & BNR hotels and the same was got published in Times of India, Delhi, Mumbai, Ahmadabad, Kolkata. As per this NIT, the sale of tender document for RYN was to form 18.10.2006 to 09.11.2006 with date of submission upto 10.11.2006 (12:00hours) and opening of bid of documents on 10.11.2006(12:15 hours).As per this NIT the sale of tender document for BNR Hotels was to be start from 23.10.2006 to 16.11.2006 with date of submission upto17.11.2006 (12:00 hours) and opening of bid documents on 17.11.2006 (1215 hours). However, in this NIT, it was wrongly printed that party should be in the business of operating and maintaining hotel (at least a 2-star category) for the last three financial years, instead of five years, as approved by the MD, IRCTC as mentioned above and also as reflected in the advertisement dated 03.11.2006.

19. That on 01.11.2006, Sh. Rakesh Saksena moved a proposal for extension of the date for sale of tender documents for Budget Hotels as well as four IRCTC

properties. It was proposed that the date for IRCTC properties (including BNR Hotels) was to be extended upto 30.11.2006 and date of submission of bids to 01.12.2006. This note mentions that:

> "IRCTC is conducting Road Shows at several locations to garner large-scale support for the Budget Hotel project. Road Shows have already been planned in Chennai, Tirupati, Jaipur, Bhopal and other locations.
>
> In addition, FHRAI, the leading federation of the hotel industry is conducting its Annual Convention at Chandigarh from 10th Nov. to 12th Nov., 2006. IRCTC will be participating in the convention to canvass support for the concept of Budget Hotels".

This note was approved by Sh. P.K. Goel on 01.11.2006. Accordingly, further advertisement was published on 03.11.2006 in leading newspapers which clearly mentioned that the eligibility criteria included at least 2-Star category for the last 5 financial years. The abovesaid note clearly mentions that Road Shows and attendance at FHRAI conference was to garner support for Budget Hotels. There is no mention of Rail Yatri Niwas or BNR Hotels in this note. It is established that BNR Hotels were different from Budget Hotels in as much as BNR Hotels were existing properties whereas Budget Hotels were a mega developing concept which was yet to materialize.

20. That pursuant to the criminal conspiracy and to favour M/s Sujata Hotels Pvt. Ltd., on 13.11.2006, Shri Rakesh Saksena initiated a note for amendment of eligibility conditions in respect of BNR Hotels.

The proposal relaxed the eligibility criteria on the following three issues:-

(i) Turnover criteria of Rs. 3 crore was retained with the modification for its being only last 02 financial years (2004-05 & 2005-06) as against earlier for 03 years i.e. (2003-04, 2004-05 & 2005-06)

(ii) The clause of operating and maintaining 02 Star category hotel or equivalent type property with food facility for last 02 financial years (2004-05 & 2005-06) as against earlier for the last 05 financial years.

(iii) Certificate of Star classification/reclassification for the hotel operated/managed by the bidder issued by competent authority was modified to certificate of Star classification/reclassification issued by competent authority or self certificate that the property is equivalent to at least 02 Star or above category, if official classification has not been taken/or is applied for.

The aforesaid changes were only restricted to Rail Yatri Niwas and BNR Hotels (not Budget Hotels) for which there was no explanation or justification in any file or statement, though widcr participation should have been invited/encouraged for the 100 budget hotels all over the country and not restricted to four existing BNR Hotels. This note was put up through Sh. Gogia, the then Jt. GM and sc approved by Sh. P.K.Goel, the then MD. Accordingly, it corrigendum to this effect was issued on 15.11.2006.

21. That the aforesaid changes were made in the minimum eligibility criteria i.e. (i) reducing the 2 Star Category status for the last five financial year to two financial

years and (ii) and certification to this effect which was to be issued by competent authority was modified to the certification either by competent authority or self-certification with a dishonest intention to suit the needs of M/s Sujata Hotels Pvt Ltd as otherwise M/s Sujata Hotels Pvt. Ltd. would not have been eligible for this tender as per the eligibility criteria approved by the then MD IRCTC on 06.10.2006 and the criteria published in the advertisement dated 03.11.2006. It was only subsequent to this corrigendum that M/s Sujata Hotels Pvt. Ltd. submitted its bid. It is further established that neither any road show as regards BNR hotels was conducted nor any feedback regarding BNR hotels was received during abovesaid FHRAI convention at Chandigarh, which took place from 10 to 12 November 2006. The purpose of road shows and participation in FHRAI Conference was already spelt out by Sh. Saksena in his note dated 01.11.2006 wherein he had specifically written that these were done for Budget Hotels. There is no mention of BNR Hotels in that note. Therefore, the justification for changing the tender conditions for BNR Hotels were found to be

false and baseless and the same was done with the malafide intention of favouring M/s Sujata Hotels Pvt. Ltd.

22. That it was pursuant to the conspiracy that the note for date of extension of submission of bids and changes in the tender conditions was initiated directly at the level of Sh. Rakesh Saksena whereas majority of the proposals at IRCTC have been initiated by the subordinate rank officers.

23. That it was claimed that 15 tender documents in

respect of BNR Hotel Ranchi and 17 tender documents in respect of BNR Hotel Puri were sold, but the details of only 2 out of 15 parties in respect of BNR Hotel Ranchi and 5 out of 17 parties in respect of BNR hotel Puri(total 07 parties only) are on record. It is established during investigation that some parties which were shown to have purchased the tender documents had not purchased any tender document from IRCTC in respect of BNR Hotels at Ranchi & Puri.

24. That apart from M/s Sujata Hotels Pvt. Ltd., which submitted its bid for both BNR Hotels Ranchi and Puri, there was only one other bidder for BNR Ranchi and one for BNR Puri who had submitted their bids. In respect of BNR Ranchi, the bidder other than M/s Sujata Hotels Pvt. Ltd. had submitted the bid on the telephonic instructions of RJD Party Leader, who had threatened him to quote the rates between Rs. 4 to 5 crores as an amount of licence fee to be paid by the bidder. Due to fear and insecurity, this bidder submitted his tender documents and quoted the rates as told to him.

25. That as per the advertisement, the bids were to be opened on 01.12.2006 at 1215 PM in the office of IRCTC in the presence of all the bidders who had participated. But both the bidders other than M/s Sujata Hotels Pvt. Ltd. were made to sign some papers before the scheduled time of opening of bids. It was told by the IRCTC officials that it had been decided that tender would not be opened on that day as ordered by the top most official of IRCTC. They thereafter directed to leave the IRCTC office stating that they would be informed about the date

of opening of the tender.

26. That no officer/official of IRCTC was nominated for opening of the bids. However, the bids are shown to have been opened on 01.12.2006 by two subordinate officials of IRCTC, on the verbal instructions of Shri B.K Agarwal and Shri R.K. Gogia without any written orders or approval in the relevant file. It is revealed that the names of these two subordinate officials were considered on file vide notings dated 05.12.2006 for initial screening. There is another note dated 01.12.2006 initiated by Sh. P.K. Goel, the then MD IRCTC himself wherein he formed a Tender Committee comprising of Sh. Vinod Asthana the then GGM (Operations), Sh. B.K. Agrawal, the then GGM (Tourism Services) and Sh. R.K. Gogia, the then JGM (Finance) & Company Secretary. Strangely, Sh. P.K. Goel, MD did not put any date under his signatures on this note which was acknowledged by the aforesaid officials on 02.12.2006. It is revealed that the noting dated 05.12.2006 as mentioned above, are placed below the notings dated 02.12.2006 but before noting dated 04.12.2006 on the next page, revealing ante dating of these records.

27. That the Tender Committee did not use the criteria for evaluation of technical bids as mentioned in the tender documents. It introduced/exercised a revised threshold based criteria for the purpose, which was in violation of CVC circular No.33/7/03 dated 09.07.2003 which mentions that evaluation criteria not stipulated in the bid documents vitiate the sanctity of tender system and whatever evaluation criteria which the organization wants to adopt should be made explicit at the time of inviting tenders so

that basic concept of transparency and interests of equity and fairness are satisfied. There is nothing on record to suggest as to at what stage after the opening of bids the new threshold for evaluation of bids was introduced (as the same was not part of tender documents) and who recorded the approval for the same. At the instance of the Tender Committee the proforma/columns used for initial screening of the technical bids was mischievously designed so as to conceal the status of property of M/S Sujata Hotel Pvt. Ltd., for the last two financial years 2004-05&2005-06, which was one of the eligibility criteria. It is on the basis of this subsequently introduced new evaluation standard that the Tender Committee awarded the marks in an arbitrary fashion leading to the technical rejection of the second bidder in respect of BNR Hotel Puri as it was awarded 53 marks out of 100 whereas the minimum bench mark for qualification was kept at 60. It is on record that despite the fact that M/s Sujata Hotels Pvt. Ltd., did not submit any document regarding its Star category status of the preceding two years nor gave any self certification to this effect, the Tender Committee deliberately and with the malafide intention overlooked this mandatory requirement without any deliberation.

28. That on 23.12.2006, the Tender Committee recommendations in favour of M/s Sujata Hotels Pvt. Ltd. were accepted by Shri P.K. Goel, the then MD, IRCTC. Letter of awards of lease for BNR hotels at Ranchi & Puri in favour of M/s Sujata Hotel Pvt. Ltd., Patna, were issued by the IRCTC on 27.12.2006.

29. That the aforesaid facts establish that the whole process of award of contract in respect of BNR Hotels

at Ranchi and Puri was rigged and manipulated in favour of M/s Sujata Hotels Pvt. Ltd. in the absence of other two participants in the tender process as mentioned above.

30. That investigation has revealed that 358 Decimal of land was sold by Kochhar brothers to M/s DMCPL for a consideration of Rs. 1.61 crores through 11 sale deeds all executed on 25.02.2005. The land was shown to be an agricultural land in the Sale Deed and the stamp duty was collected as per the lowest slab of Rs. 45,000/- per Decimal which was fixed for Residential Inside Road Category as per the rates notified by Govt. of Bihar. Since, the plots are found to have been situated at main road i.e. Bailey Road, the circle rate applicable was Rs. 55,000/- per Decimal. The value of the land as per the Circle Rate should be a minimum of Rs. 1.96 crores. Therefore, the sale was affected at a lower price than what was fixed by the Government for that area. It has been established that there was no land which was categorized as agricultural land in Mauja Jalalpur, Patna at that time. The plots in question were located on the main Bailey Road Patna as such minimum category of circle rate under which registry to be made as on 25.02.2005 was Residential Main Road Category i.e. Rs 55000/-. Thus the total sale consideration of five plots should have been Rs 1,96,90,000/- (358 decimal x RS 55000/-) and thus a difference in sale consideration comes to Rs 35,23,000/- (1,96,90,000-1,61,67,000/-). Therefore an additional duty of Rs-6,13,002/- (17.4% of 35,23,000/-) was required to be paid on account of difference in sale consideration of properties in question.

31. That in 2005-06, this land was considered to be a prime property account of its location on 286 feet wide Bailey Road Patna around which rapid commercial growth was taking place. The significance of the property is further evident from the fact that in2005 the Circle Rate of the property situated on Bailey Road Patna under Jalalpur Mouza was ranging from Rs. 55000-65000 per decimal whereas the circle rate of the property situated on main Bailey Road in the year 2014 was Rs. 24,00,000/- and 21,60,000/- per decimal and at present the Circle Rate is Rs.26,00,000/- per decimal and is categorized as commercial. Therefore, as per the prevailing circle rate, the total value of the land till 09.10.2014 was Rs. 85.92 crores and the present value of the land is Rs. 93.08 crores.
32. That M/s Delight Marketing Company Private Limited (M/s DMCPL) was incorporated on 10.06.1981 by Late Harish Chander Bhasin and Shri Prem Gupta (Now member of Parliament Rajya Sabha and commonly known as Prem Chand Gupta or P.C. Gupta) and both of them were first Directors of the company. The current account of M/s DMCPL was opened with State Bank of India, Main Branch, Parliament Street, New Delhi by Shri Prem Chand Gupta on 09.06.1981 and he had signed the said account opening form as Secretary / Managing Agent of the company. He was also the authorized signatory of the bank account of the company, maintained with State Bank of India, Main Branch, New Delhi. Thus it is clear that initially the company M/s DMCPL was formed and run by Shri Prem Chand Gupta and all the operations of the company were being looked after by him only. Sh.

Prem Chand Gupta is a close associate of Sh. Lalu Prasad Yadav and has been continuously elected as Member of Parliament since 1997 on being nominated by Rashtriya Janta Dal of which Sh. Lulu Prasad Yadav is the founder President. After joining politics, Sh. Prem Chand Gupta resigned from company. However, indirect control over all the functions of companies/ group companies remained with him and his wife Smt. Sarla Gupta. This is evident from the fact that the company issued 4000 equity shares of Rs100/- each aggregating to Rs 4,00,000/-and increased its paid up capital to the Rs 400200/- in the year 1994-1995 but these 4000 equity shares were allotted to the persons, most of whom were either the employees of the group companies of Sh. P.C. Gupta or his family members.

33. That in pursuance of criminal conspiracy, in a pre planned manner, Smt. Sarla Gupta acquired around 71% shares of M/s DMCPL, either in her name or in the name of her controlled companies, just before acquisition of land at Patna on 25.02.2005, so that the control over the company should vest with her. Most of the share transfers took place on 10.02.2005 &14.02.005 i.e. around 15-20 days before purchase of abovesaid land in the name of the company.

34. That in the year 2005, Shri Prem Chand Gupta, using his influence arranged a loan/advance of Rs2 Crores/- from M/s Abhishek Finance Company Ltd. and purchased the abovesaid land for M/s DMCPL from Kochhars, against a consideration of Rs1.61 Crores. The sale deed for purchase of aforesaid land at Patna on behalf of the company was signed by Late Shri M.L. Rustagi, the then one of directors of the Company,

who was also an employee of the company. Shri Prem Chand Gupta is Member of Parliament (Rajya Sabha) from the State of Jharkhand from last fifteen years and is a permanent resident of New Delhi and all his family members also reside in Delhi. After purchase of said land at Patna in the name of M/s DMCPL, neither was any other land purchased at Patna (by any of the companies owned/controlled by Sh. P.C. Gupta and his family members) nor this land was used by the company for any purpose. It thus clearly shows that the purchase of abovesaid land was arranged by Shri P.C. Gupta and his wife Smt. Sarla Gupta, in the name of one of their controlled companies namely M/s DMCPL, pursuant to the criminal conspiracy.

35. That after purchase of abovesaid land by M/s DMCPL, all the shares of the company were transferred to the close associates of Shri P.C. Gupta and Smt. Sarla Gupta, so that the control over the assets of company including the said land remained vested with them only. It is revealed that 190000 preference shares were issued by the company to the persons known to Shri P.C. Gupta/ Smt. Sarla Gupta or arranged through their dose associates, with a false promise diversification of business activities of the company and a good return against the investment. This way, the company generated an amount of around Rs1.9 Crores from different persons/companies, but no return was given to them even after a lapse of a period of 2-3 years (at the time of buy back of the preference shares). This clearly shows that the preference shares were issued by M/s DMCPL in order to generate funds, with an object to clear the loan taken from M/s Abhishek

Finance Company. In fact, no business activities was conducted or expanded by M/s DMCPL during this period. Later, in order to gain profit out of long term capital gain, a loan of Rs 50 lakhs was taken by M/s DMCPL from M/s Lubetec India (Pvt) Ltd. and the same was invested inequity shares of M/s Ahluwalia Contracts India Ltd on 02.12.2008.These shares were offloaded on 21.12.2009 & 23.12.2009 by generating huge profit in the books of company, as a long term capital gain. There was abnormal rise of around 627% in price of the shares of M/s Ahluwalia Contracts India Ltd, when the same were sold by M/s DMCPL in the market. After getting huge profit to the tune of around Rs.2.68 Crores, the optionally convertible preference shares of the company was bought back from the concerned preference shares holder. However, no dividend or profit was given to any of the investors by M/s DMCPL.

36. That during 2004, entire 4002 shares of M/s DMCPL were held by employees of the group companies of Shri Prem Chand Gupta.
37. That this shareholding pattern underwent a change after acquisition of the mentioned property at Patna. While the number of shareholders came down, the majority shareholding consolidated in the hands of Ms. Sarla Gupta and her two companies.
38. That one share of M/s DMCPL, held by Shri Harish Chander Bhasin, initial Director of the company was transferred to Shri Tejaswi Prasad Yadav in 2011, though no record in this regard is available.
39. That Ms. Sarla Gupta w/o Shri Prem Chand Gupta transferred 1500 of her shares of M/s DMCPL to Ms. Rabri Devi in the year 2010 for Rs. 75 lakhs. This

purchase was financed by her through the money received from Shri Amrendra Kumar Sinha, Proprietor of M/s Shreya Construction in lieu of development agreement for plots of land owned by her. In respect of one of these plots of land, it is revealed that though the transfer deed is dated 09.12.2005, the consideration for the same was paid in 1980 i.e. 25 years prior to registration of the sale deed.

40. That Ms. Rabri Devi further acquired 1101 shares of this company from Ms. Sarla Gupta in the year 2014 for Rs. 63.30 lakhs, which come to Rs. 5750/- (approx) per share. She also acquired 750 shares of this company from M/s IST Technology & Infrastructure Pvt Ltd. in the year 2014 for approx. Rs. 43.12 lakhs. For purchase of these shares, she received Rs. 1 crore on 06.02.2014 from the joint account of her daughter and son-in-law.

41. That during the same time, Shri Tejaswi Prasad Yadav acquired 650 shares of this company from the shareholders of M/s DMCPL for Rs. 1.30 lakhs i.e. @ Rs. 200/- per share, paid in cash, who were all employees of Shri Prem Chand Gupta or his group companies.

42. That S/Shri Vijay Pal Tripathi, Deoki Nandan Tulshyan, N.M. Kakrania and Gokul Singh, are shareholders of M/s DMPCL have claimed to be employees of the companies of Shri Prem Chand Gupta. They have pleaded ignorance w.r.t. these financial transactions and admitted having signed the financial documents on the directions of Shri Prem Chand Gupta.

43. That it is relevant to mention that while Ms. Rabri Devi purchased the shares of thye same company at the rate of Rs. 5750/- per share, shri Tejaswui Prasad

Yadav did so only @Rs. 200/- share.

44. That after Shri Lalu Prasad demitted office, the process of transfer of shares of M/s DMCPL to his family members started w.e.f. 31.05.2010 and culminated in February, 2014, with Ms. Rabri Devi and Shri Tejaswi Yadav coming into possession of entire 4002 shares. The complete control of the company was taken by the family members of Shri Lalu Prasad Yadav by the year 2014 with the appointment of Shri Tej Pratap Yadav and Ms. Chanda Yadav as Directors of the company on 29.09.2014. The name of the company was thereafter changed to M/s Lara Projects Pvt Ltd w.e.f. 22.11.2016. In January 2017, the company i.e. M/s LARA Projects Pvt. Ltd. was converted into M/s LARA Projects LLP. There were three designated partners of M/s LARA Projects LLP namely Smt. Rabri Devi having 60% obligation and Shri Tej Pratap Yadav and Shri Tejashwi Prasad Yadav having 20% each.

The facts as disclosed above i.e. the rigged and manipulated tender process of award of re-development/ operation of two Railway properties to M/s Sujata Hotels Pvt. Ltd., sale of land by M/s Sujata Hotels Pvt. Ltd. (to whom licence was awarded) to M/s DMCPL which was later controlled by family members of the then Railway Minister at much lower price and subsequent transfer of ownership of this company to the family members of the then Railway Minister at a throw away price establish the fact that Sh. Lalu Prasad Yadav, the then Railway Minister equipped with the knowledge about transfer of BNR Hotels at Ranchi and Puri for its management, conspired with the officials of IRCTC, promoters of M/s Sujata Hotels Pvt. Ltd. and the Directors of M/s DMCPL to derive undue pecuniary benefit through his wife Smt. Rabri Devi and son Shri Tejashwi Yaday. The property in question was bought in the name of M/s DMCPL controlled by Sh. P.C. Gupta and was held by him for the ultimate benefit of Sh. Lalu Prasad Yadav and his family members.

The facts, findings, circumstances and the reasoning, as discussed above, disclose commission of offences punishable u/s 120-B r/w 420 IPC, Sec 13(2) r/w 13(1) (d) of the PC Act, 1988 and substantive offences thereof, on part of accused persons namely Shri Lalu Prasad Yadav (A-1), Smt. Rabri Devi Yadav w/o Shri Lalu Prasad Yadav (A-2), Shri Tejashwi Prasad Yadav s/o Shri Lalu Prasad Yadav (A-3), M/s LARA Projects LLP (erstwhile known as M/s Lara Projects Pvt. Ltd./ M/s Delight Marketing Company Pvt. Ltd.) (A-4), Shri Vijay Kochar (A-5), Shri Vinay Kochhar (A-6), Smt. Sarla Gupta w/o Shri Prem Chand Gupta (A-7), Shri P. K. Goel, the then Managing Director, IRCTC, (Now retd.) (A-8) (all FIR named accused persons) and Shri Prem Chand Gupta, a sitting Member of Parliament (Rajya Sabha) (A-9), Shri Rakesh Saksena, the then Director, (T&M), IRCTC (Now retd.) (A-10), Shri B.K. Agarwal, the then GGM (Tourism Services), IRCTC (presently working as Additional Member (PU), Railway Board, Ministry of Railway, Govt. of India) New Delhi (A-11), Shri R.K. Gogia, the then JGM & CS, IRCTC (A-12), Shri V.K. Asthana, the then GGM (Operation), IRCTC (A-13), M/s Sujata Hotel Pvt. Ltd. Hotels Pvt. Ltd. through its directors (A-14).

It is therefore prayed that accused persons, as named above, may please

be summoned and tried according to law for the offences punishable u/s 120-B

r/w 420 IPC, Sec 13 (2) r/w 13 (1) (d) of PC Act of 1988 and substantive offences thereof.

The sanction for prosecution U/s 19 of PC Act 1988

in respect of Sh. B.K. Agrawal, the then GGM (Tourism Services), IRCTC, presently working as Additional Member Railway Board, Ministry of Railway is being obtained. No

sanction is required in respect of other accused public servants, as they have since retired from service.

Further, it is intimated that further investigation under the provisions of Sec. 173(8) Cr.PC, is in progress and a due report to this effect shall be submitted to this Hon'ble Court in due course.

18. Refer Notice served	:	
19. Dispatched on	:	16.04.2018 vide No.
20. No. of Enclosures	:	02 (two) i.e. Annexure 'A' & 'B'
21. List of Enclosures	:	List of Witnesses (Annexure - 'A') List of Documents (Annexure - 'B')

SIGNATURE OF THE
INVESTIGATING OFFICER
SUBMITTING THE REPORT

(SANJAY DUBEY)
DY. SP OF POLICE
CBI, EO-II, NEW DELHI
(INVESTIGATING OFFICER)

FORWARDED BY

SUPDT. OF POLICE
CBI, EO-II, NEW DELHI

□

मिट्टी घोटाला :
मुफ्त के आम, गुठलियों के दाम

पटना की जिस जमीन पर तेजस्वी प्रसाद यादव के महामॉल का निर्माण सुरसंड से राजद के विधायक सैयद अबू दोजाना की कंपनी मेरीडियन कंस्ट्रक्शन (इंडिया) प्रा.लि. द्वारा कराया जा रहा था, उसके दो अंडरग्राउंड फ्लोर की मिट्टी को पटना स्थित संजय गांधी जैविक उद्यान को बेच दिया गया। पटना का संजय गांधी जैविक उद्यान पर्यावरण एवं वन विभाग के अंतर्गत आता है, जिसके तत्कालीन मंत्री लालू प्रसाद के बड़े पुत्र और तेजस्वी प्रसाद यादव के बड़े भाई तेज प्रताप यादव थे।

चिड़ियाखाना में मॉल के दो अंडरग्राउंड फ्लोर की खपाई गई मिट्टी

- मॉल की मिट्टी को खपाने के लिए जैविक उद्यान में अनावश्यक पगडंडी (Pathway) बनाने तथा सौंदर्यीकरण के नाम पर 95.75 लाख रुपए का एक प्राक्कलन तैयार किया गया।
- वर्ष 2012 में एयरपोर्ट अथॉरिटी ने चिड़ियाघर के Funnel area में पेड़ों की कटाई के समय कुछ सुझाव दिए थे, जिसको आधार बनाकर पाँच साल बाद मिट्टी के पथ का प्राक्कलन तैयार किया गया।
- बिहार वित्त (संशोधन) नियमावली, 2016 के अनुसार, 5 लाख रुपए से अधिक की खरीद निविदा के माध्यम से कराने का प्रावधान है; परंतु 95.75 लाख रुपए का पथ निर्माण कार्य बिना टेंडर के कोटेशन के आधार पर आमंत्रित किया गया।
- मिट्टी खरीद के सभी पाँच कोटेशंस 23 अगस्त, 2016 को एक ही दिन प्राप्त हुए।
- कोटेशंस देनेवाली सभी एजेंसियों द्वारा मिट्टी की दरशाई गई दर क्रमशः 4,500/4,600/4,700/4,800/एवं 5,000/ प्रति हाइवा थी। प्रारंभ की चार दरों में 100–100 रुपए का अंतर है तथा अंतिम दो दरों में 200 रुपए का अंतर है।
- कोटेशन की दरों को देखने पर लगता है कि कोटेशन को मैनेज कर कार्य आवंटित किया गया।
- अगस्त 2016 में मिट्टी पथ निर्माण के प्राक्कलन के औचित्य पर कहा गया है—"दर्शकों की संख्या में वृद्धि और भविष्य में होनेवाली संभावित वृद्धि को ध्यान में रखकर प्रस्तावित पथ केवल दर्शकों के पैदल प्रयोग के लिए होगा।"
- परंतु सरकार द्वारा गठित जाँच समिति के समक्ष औचित्य के अंतर्गत दर्शकों की संख्या का हवाला छोड़कर वर्ष 2012 के AAI के सुझाव, निगरानी कार्य तथा अग्नि सुरक्षा कार्य का हवाला दिया जाने लगा।
- पाथ–वे के विभिन्न भागों की ऊँचाई जान–बूझकर 4 फीट, 3 फीट एवं 2 फीट रखी गई, ताकि अत्यधिक मिट्टी को खपाया जा सके।

- चिड़ियाघर में सूर्यास्त के बाद निर्माण कार्य कराने पर रोक है, उसके बावजूद 904 ट्रिप हाइवा से मिट्टी ढुलाई का कार्य रात में किया गया।
- मिट्टी की आपूर्ति हेतु M/S Enterprises को 35 लाख रुपए एवं बोल्डर हेतु मेसर्स वीरेंद्र कुमार सिंह, बुद्धा कॉलोनी को 18 लाख 36 हजार रुपए का भुगतान किया गया।
- हकीकत यह है कि तेजस्वी के मॉल की मिट्टी को खपाने के लिए पूरा ताना–बाना तैयार किया गया और एक मिट्टी घोटाले को अंजाम दिया गया।

ए.के. इन्फोसिस्टम्स प्रा.लि.

हर काम के लिए जमीन

तुम मुझे जमीन दो, मैं तुम्हारा काम करूँगा।

जमीन के बदले काम—लालू का नारा

- राबड़ी सरकार के कार्यकाल (2000-2005) के दौरान ओमप्रकाश कत्याल एवं अमित कत्याल की कंपनी आइसबर्ग इंडस्ट्रीज प्रा.लि. ने बिहटा में शराब की फैक्टरी लगाई। आइसबर्ग में लालू की बेटी चंदा यादव भी डायरेक्टर थी।
- 28 सितंबर, 2006 को ए.के. इन्फोसिस्टम्स प्रा.लि. नाम की कंपनी गठित हुई, जिसमें श्री अमित कत्याल, भाई राजेश कत्याल एवं अन्य डायरेक्टर थे।
- इस कंपनी में श्री तेजस्वी प्रसाद यादव, श्री तेज प्रताप यादव, चंदा यादव एवं रागिनी लालू जून 2014 से डायरेक्टर नियुक्त किए गए।
- आज इस कंपनी के 100 प्रतिशत शेयर्स राबड़ी देवी एवं तेजस्वी यादव के पास हैं।
- आज इस कंपनी के पास पटना शहर में करोड़ों की जमीन है, जिसका पूरा मालिकाना हक लालू परिवार के पास है।
- कत्याल परिवार को बिहार में शराब फैक्टरी लगाने में मदद करने के एवज में लालू परिवार को करोड़ों की जमीन कत्याल परिवार ने सौंप दी।
- श्री अमित कत्याल ने मात्र 50 हजार रुपए में राबड़ी देवी को तथा राजेश कत्याल ने भी 50 हजार रुपए में राबड़ी देवी एवं तेजस्वी यादव को अपने सारे शेयर्स दे दिए।

- 31 मार्च, 2007 को 50 लाख 39 हजार रुपए में पटना के दानापुर में तथा वर्ष 2011-12 में पटना में 68 लाख रुपए में एक और जमीन खरीदी गई।
- अमित कत्याल की एक अन्य कंपनी फ्रॉस्ट फाल्कन डिस्टिलरीज प्रा.लि. (Frost Falcon Distilleries Pvt.Ltd.) तथा आइसबर्ग इंडस्ट्रीज (Iceberg Industries) ने ए.के. इन्फोसिस्टम्स प्रा.लि. को 80 लाख रुपए का कर्ज दिया।
- वर्ष 2014-15 में कंपनी तेजस्वी यादव को ट्रांसफर कर दी गई, परंतु यह पैसा कभी वापस नहीं किया गया।
- श्री तेजस्वी यादव को अमित कत्याल की कंपनी ट्रिएंगल ट्रेडिंग लि. (Triangle Trading Ltd.) के द्वारा वर्ष 2010 में 9.5 लाख रुपयों की गाड़ी उपलब्ध कराई गई।
- अमित कत्याल लालू प्रसाद के दामाद शैलेश कुमार तथा बेटी मीसा भारती के साथ मेसर्स किंगडम होटल एंड रिसोर्ट प्रा.लि. (M/s Kingdom Hotel & Resort Pvt. Ltd.) में वर्ष 2006 से 2009 तक डायरेक्टर थे।
- अमित कत्याल ने तेजस्वी को 30.26 लाख रुपए तथा तेज प्रताप को 55.51 लाख रुपए कर्ज दिए, जिसे बाद में Write Off कर दिया गया।
- इसी प्रकार अमित कत्याल की कंपनी कृष रिएलिटी निर्माण प्रा.लि. (Krish Reality Nirman Pvt. Ltd.)की फर्जी बुक में मीसा भारती को 2.7 लाख रुपए ब्रॉकरेज दिखाया गया है, जो केवल बुक एंट्री है।

इस प्रकार, कत्याल परिवार ने लालू परिवार को उपकृत करने के लिए ए.के. इन्फोसिस्टम्स का गठन किया। जमीन खरीदने के लिए 1 करोड़ 48 लाख रुपए दिए और फिर जमीन सहित पूरी कंपनी तेजस्वी-राबड़ी को सौंप दी।

सवाल है कि—

- आखिर कत्याल परिवार ने लालू के बेटों व बेटियों को डायरेक्टर क्यों बनाया ?
- आखिर क्यों कत्याल परिवार डायरेक्टर पद से हट गए और केवल लालू परिवार के लोग ही पद पर रह गए?
- आखिर क्यों कत्याल परिवार ने अपने सारे शेयर्स राबड़ी और तेजस्वी को ट्रांसफर कर दिए?
- आखिर क्यों कत्याल परिवार ने जमीन खरीदी और कुछ वर्षों के बाद जमीन सहित पूरी कंपनी लालू परिवार को सौंप दी?
- तेजस्वी व राबड़ी बताएँ कि केवल 1 लाख रुपए निवेश कर वे करोड़ों की संपत्ति वाली कंपनी के मालिक कैसे बन गए?

□

फेयर ग्रो होल्डिंग्स प्रा.लि.

टाटा स्टील के दो मंजिला मकान के मालिक बन गए तेजस्वी

एक और खोखा कंपनी फेयर ग्रो होल्डिंग्स प्रा.लि. तेजस्वी यादव के कब्जे में है। इसके माध्यम से टाटा स्टील की पटना की प्राइम लोकेशन पर अवस्थित करोड़ों की संपत्ति हथिया ली गई। छह अन्य मुखौटा कंपनियों के माध्यम से करोड़ों की बेनामी संपत्ति खरीदकर पूरी कंपनी पर तेजस्वी यादव के परिवार ने कब्जा जमा लिया।

- श्री लालू प्रसाद ने अपने दोनों बेटों—तेजस्वी, तेज प्रताप एवं बेटियों चंदा यादव, रागिनी लालू को पटना शहर के अत्यंत महँगे इलाके बेली रोड के सटे टाटा स्टील के दो मंजिला गेस्ट हाउस का मालिक बनाने के लिए राबड़ी देवी के मुख्यमंत्रित्व काल (वर्ष 2000-05) के दौरान सहारा समूह एवं प्रेमचंद गुप्ता से जुड़े लोगों की मुखौटा कंपनी फेयर ग्रो होल्डिंग्स प्रा.लि. (Fairgrow Holdings Pvt. Ltd.) का भरपूर इस्तेमाल किया।
- पटना के 5, राइडिंग रोड (केंद्रीय विद्यालय बेली रोड के सामने) में 7,105 वर्ग फीट (5 कट्ठा, 4 धुर एवं 8 धुरकी) मुख्य सड़क पर निर्मित 5,348 वर्ग फीट के दो मंजिला पक्का मकान, जो एक जमाने में TISCO का गेस्ट हाउस हुआ करता था, उसे फेयर ग्रो होल्डिंग्स प्रा.लि. नामक मुखौटा कंपनी के माध्यम से अपने कब्जे में ले लिया।
- उपर्युक्त 7,105 वर्ग फीट एवं दो मंजिला मकान का ब्योरा निम्न है—

  खाता नं.-461, 446/410, 445

  प्लॉट नं. 1775, 1780, 1781, 1782

शेखपुरा थाना-शास्त्रीनगर, पी.एम.सी. वार्ड नं.-33 सर्किल नं.-247 होल्डिंग नं. 666/129A

- उपर्युक्त जमीन पर 5,348 वर्गफीट का दो मंजिला मकान है, जिसमें—

Ground Floor

- RR Office Room
- Visitors Lounge
- 3 Officers Room
- 1 Kitchen Room
- 2 Drawing Room
- 1 Dining Room

First Floor

- Supervisor Room
- Stair Case
- Guest House
- 3 Bed Room with Bath Room & Lounge
- Out House Area
- Store Room (South House)

□

5 राइडिंग रोड, पटना स्थित टाटा स्टील से प्राप्त तेजस्वी यादव की संपत्ति

इस शानदार मकान में निम्न करोड़ों की संपत्ति के भी मालिक हैं तेजस्वी

Tube light	16
Ceiling Fan	25
Red woollen Carpet	8
Window Pulment Fitting	5
Fancy Light Bulb with Cover	23
Ceiling Light Fitting	11
Wall Mirror in Bath Room	5
Vapour Light Fitting	4
झूमर काँच का (बड़ा)	4

Wardrobe With mirror & Cabinet	4
Wooden Book Self Fitted in wall	1
Curtain Rod door	13
Geyser	04
Exhaust Fan	02

- पंद्रह वर्षों के बाद भी रजिस्टर-2 पर रैयत के रूप में TISCO का ही नाम दर्ज है, जो वर्ष 1988-89 में दर्ज हुआ था।
- आखिर पंद्रह वर्षों के बाद भी रजिस्टर-2 में TISCO का नाम हटाकर फेयर ग्रो का नाम क्यों नहीं दर्ज किया गया?

संपत्ति खरीदने के लिए फर्जी कंपनी का इस्तेमाल

- आखिर तेजस्वी, तेज प्रताप फेयर ग्रो जैसी मुखौटा कंपनी के डायरेक्टर क्यों बने?
- तेजस्वी परिवार यदि TISCO की संपत्ति सीधे खरीदता तो लोगों को बताना पड़ता कि इसे खरीदने के लिए पैसा कहाँ से आया?
- इसलिए फेयर ग्रो जैसी मुखौटा कंपनी को TISCO की संपत्ति खरीदने के लिए मुखौटे के रूप में इस्तेमाल किया गया।
- फेयर ग्रो होल्डिंग कंपनी का रजिस्टर्ड पता 130/1, बाकुल बगान रोड, थाना-भवानीपुर, कोलकाता दिखाया गया है; जबकि इस पते पर इस नाम की कोई कंपनी नहीं पाई गई।
- वर्ष 2009 में इस कंपनी के 15 शेयर होल्डर्स का पता अलग अलग, 2 गणेश चंद्र एवेन्यू, 26 पी.के. टैगोर स्ट्रीट एवं 9 मेंगो स्ट्रीट, कोलकाता दिखाया गया है; परंतु उपर्युक्त पते पर कोई शेयर्स होल्डर नहीं पाया गया।
- इसी प्रकार पाँच कंपनियों (सहारा मर्चेंडाइज प्रा.लि. सहित) के नाम 20-20 हजार के शेयर दिखलाए गए हैं तथा इन सभी कंपनियों का पता 85, मेटकाल स्ट्रीट, कोलकाता दिखलाया गया।

- जाँच के दौरान इस पते पर कोई कंपनी नहीं पाई गई।
- वर्ष 2016 में इन सभी शेयर होल्डर्स (16 व्यक्ति और 5 कंपनियों) का नया पता 130/1 बाकुल बगान रोड दिखलाया गया, जो पूर्णतया फर्जी है।
- इस कंपनी में न तो कोई कर्मचारी है, न ही कोई व्यवसाय है और न ही कोई टर्नओवर है।

आखिर किस काबिलीयत पर तेजस्वी बने डायरेक्टर?

- इस कंपनी की आज तक कभी वार्षिक आम सभा क्यों नहीं हुई?
- फिर ऐसी फर्जी कंपनी, जिसके रजिस्टर्ड पते से लेकर शेयर होल्डर्स तक सभी फर्जी हैं, उसके डायरेक्टर वर्ष 2014 में तेजस्वी, तेज प्रताप, चंदा यादव, रागिनी लालू कैसे बन गए?
- आखिर इन्हें डायरेक्टर किसने नियुक्त किया; जबकि सभी शेयर होल्डर्स फर्जी हैं?
- तेजस्वी हाई स्कूल फेल एवं तेज प्रताप मात्र इंटर पास हैं। फिर इनकी किस काबिलीयत को देखकर इन्हें डायरेक्टर बनाया गया?
- केवल टिस्को की संपत्ति खरीदने के लिए फेयर ग्रो जैसी बंद पड़ी कंपनी का मुखौटे के रूप में इस्तेमाल किया गया।
- इस फेयर ग्रो कंपनी को राजद सांसद और पूर्व केंद्रीय मंत्री श्री प्रेमचंद गुप्ता के परिवार के लोग फर्जी तरीके से चला रहे थे।
- श्री विजय पाल त्रिपाठी, जो फेयर ग्रो के वर्ष 2008 में डायरेक्टर थे, वे प्रेमचंद गुप्ता की कंपनी डिलाइट मार्केटिंग के भी वर्ष 2006 में निदेशक थे।
- फेयर ग्रो के एक अन्य डायरेक्टर श्री अनिल तुलस्यान सुपुत्र श्री देवकी नंदन तुलस्यान प्रेमचंद गुप्ता के चचेरे भाई हैं तथा श्री गुप्ता की अनेक कंपनियों से जुड़े रहे हैं।

टिस्को की संपत्ति तेजस्वी को देने के लिए सहारा समूह ने भुगतान किया

- TISCO की इस संपत्ति को खरीदने के लिए फेयर ग्रो के अधिकृत प्रतिनिधि के रूप में श्री राजेश कुमार सुपुत्र श्याम नारायण सिंह 33/ए, एस.के. पुरी, रोड नं.-1 पटना ने सेल डीड पर हस्ताक्षर किए हैं।
- श्री राजेश कुमार ने एस.के. पुरी का जो पता दिया है, उस पते पर राजेश कुमार नामक कोई व्यक्ति कभी नहीं रहता था, यानी राजेश कुमार का पता भी फर्जी है।
- श्री राजेश कुमार फेयर ग्रो के न तो कभी शेयर होल्डर थे, न कभी डायरेक्टर और न ही कभी कर्मचारी रहे।
- फिर श्री राजेश कुमार ने फेयरग्रो की ओर से टिस्को को 65 लाख रुपए DD No. 333760 dated 24.10.2002 Drawn on फेडरल बैंक लि. भुगतान करने के लिए पैसे कहाँ से लाए?
- श्री राजेश कुमार आखिर कौन हैं, जिन्होंने तेजस्वी खातिर टिस्को की संपत्ति खरीदने के लिए फेयर ग्रो के प्रतिनिधि बनकर 65 लाख रुपयों का भुगतान किया?
- श्री राजेश कुमार सहारा समूह के डिप्टी एम.डी. श्री जे.बी. रॉय के निजी सचिव हुआ करते थे और वर्तमान में सहारा मीडिया के कॉरपोरेट डायरेक्टर में महत्त्वपूर्ण पदाधिकारी हैं।
- फेयर ग्रो के एक समय निदेशक रहे श्री बृज सरीन और श्री यश चौधरी ने बताया कि वे राजेश कुमार के निर्देश पर बैलेंस शीट पर हस्ताक्षर करते थे तथा राजेश कुमार ने ही इनका परिचय फेयर ग्रो से कराया।
- श्री राजेश कुमार की इ-मेल आईडी rkmarcom@gmail.com पर फेयर ग्रो के अनेक निदेशक की नियुक्ति एवं त्याग-पत्र के कागज पाए गए।

- जाँच एजेंसियों को राजेश कुमार ने बताया कि सहारा ग्रुप के डी.जी. एम. श्री हरदीप सिंह के निर्देश पर वे फेयर ग्रो का काम देखते थे।
- जाँच एजेंसियों ने पाया कि राजेश कुमार फेयर ग्रो के नियमित दैनिक मामलों के कर्ता-धर्ता थे।

टाटा एवं सहारा समूह को उपकृत करने के एवज में ली गई संपत्ति

- लालू-राबड़ी अपने पंद्रह वर्षों के राज में टाटा समूह एवं सहारा समूह को अनेक प्रकार से उपकृत करते रहे, जिसके एवज में टिस्को एवं सहारा समूह ने इस संपत्ति को लालू परिवार को हासिल करवाने में मदद की।
- टाटा समूह लालू परिवार एवं राजद को पहले भी उपकृत करता रहा है। लालू की बड़ी बेटी मीसा भारती एवं रोहिणी आचार्य तथा तत्कालीन पथ निर्माण मंत्री श्री इलियास हुसैन की बेटी आसमा एवं लालू के 'कबाब मंत्री' श्री अनवर अहमद (जिनके यहाँ नोटबंदी के दौरान काले घन को सफेद करने के आरोप में सी.बी.आई. ने छापा मारा तथा उनका बेटा जेल में है) की बेटी का जमशेदपुर स्थित टाटा मेडिकल कॉलेज में नामांकन प्रतिभा के आधार पर नहीं, बल्कि टाटा के कोटे से किया गया था।
- अन्यथा TISCO फेयर ग्रो जैसी मुखौटा कंपनी को अपनी संपत्ति क्यों बेचता?
- आखिर क्यों 15 वर्षों बाद भी रजिस्टर-II में TISCO के नाम से ही संपत्ति दर्ज है और आज तक फेयर ग्रो के नाम से दाखिल-खारिज नहीं कराया गया?
- ताकि लोग यही समझते रहें कि संपत्ति TISCO की है और लालू परिवार को संपत्ति फेयर ग्रो के नाम से बेच दी गई और इस षड्यंत्र का किसी को पता नहीं चल सके?
- जाँच एजेंसियों को फेयर ग्रो की इस संपत्ति का पता लगाने में पसीने

छूट गए, क्योंकि राजेश कुमार सहित फेयर ग्रो से जुड़े सभी लोग इस संपत्ति के बारे में अनभिज्ञता जाहिर करते रहे।

- इस प्रकार, राबड़ी के मुख्यमंत्रित्व काल (2000-05) के दौरान सहारा समूह द्वारा संचालित मुखौटा कंपनी फेयर ग्रो के माध्यम से 65 लाख रुपयों का भुगतान कर TISCO की 7,105 वर्ग फीट जमीन तथा दो मंजिला मकान, जिसका वर्तमान मूल्य 10 करोड़ रुपयों से ज्यादा है, को लालू परिवार ने तेजस्वी व तेज प्रताप के लिए हासिल कर लिया है।
- 7 फरवरी, 2018 को तेजस्वी यादव की फेयर ग्रो के माध्यम से हस्तगत इस संपत्ति को Initiating officer (Benami Prohibition Unit) Patna की ओर से डॉ. प्रताप नारायण शर्मा ने Prohibition of Benami Property Transaction Act. 1988 के sub-section (3) of section 24 के अंतर्गत Provisionally attach कर लिया है।

□

ए.बी. एक्सपोर्ट्स प्रा.लि.

रंग चोखा करने का नायाब नुस्खा

- डिलाइट मार्केटिंग, ए.के. इन्फोसिस्टम और फेयर ग्रो होल्डिंग प्रा. लि. की तर्ज पर ही एक और कंपनी ए.बी. एक्सपोर्ट्स प्रा.लि. है, जिसकी शेयर होल्डिंग, डायरेक्टरशिप करोड़ों की संपत्ति सहित पूरी कंपनी पर लालू परिवार ने कब्जा कर लिया है।
- दिल्ली के सबसे पॉश इलाके में जमीन खरीदने के लिए वर्ष 2007-08 में मुंबई के पाँच बड़े ज्वेलर्स, सोने के व्यापारियों ने ए.बी. एक्सपोर्ट्स को 1 करोड़ प्रति व्यापारी कुल 5 करोड़ रुपए का कर्ज बिना ब्याज के दिया।

Alka Diamond Industries—	1 करोड़
Real Gold Trading Co. Pvt. Ltd.—	1 करोड़
Hema Trading Co. Pvt. Ltd.—	1 करोड़
Lexus Infotech Ltd.—	1 करोड़
Yash V Jewels Ltd.—	1 करोड़
	कुल : 5 करोड़

- इन 5 करोड़ रुपयों के बिना सूद के कर्ज से उसी वर्ष नई दिल्ली के D-1088, न्यू फ्रेंड्स कॉलोनी में 500 वर्ग मीटर जमीन मकान सहित 5 करोड़ रुपयों में खरीदी गई।
- आज इस जमीन की कीमत 55 करोड़ रुपए से ज्यादा है।
- इस जमीन पर लालू परिवार का चार मंजिला मकान बनकर लगभग तैयार है, जिसकी वर्तमान कीमत लगभग 60 करोड़ रुपए होगी।

- वर्ष 2010-11 में मात्र 4 लाख रुपए निवेश कर तेजस्वी यादव (98 प्रतिशत शेयर) एवं 5 हजार रुपए निवेश कर चंदा यादव (2 प्रतिशत शेयर) ने करोड़ों की संपत्ति हासिल कर ली।
- इस कंपनी के जरिए लालू परिवार नई दिल्ली में 4-5 लाख रुपए की पूँजी लगाकर 115 करोड़ रुपयों की संपत्ति का मालिक बन गया।
- रागिनी लालू तथा चंदा यादव कंपनी की डायरेक्टर हैं।
- ए.बी. एक्सपोर्ट्स में न तो कोई कर्मचारी था, न कोई व्यापार या टर्न ओवर था। इस कंपनी ने केवल तेजस्वी यादव के लिए जमीन खरीदने का एकमात्र काम किया।
- ए.बी. एक्सपोर्ट्स को कर्ज देनेवाली उपर्युक्त पाँचों कंपनियाँ कोई व्यापार नहीं करती थीं, केवल काले धन को बुक एंट्री के माध्यम से सफेद करने का काम करती थीं।
- यद्यपि श्री तेजस्वी यादव ने उप-मुख्यमंत्री बनने के एक दिन पहले 9.11.2015 को ए.बी. एक्सपोर्ट्स के डायरेक्टर पद से इस्तीफा दे दिया था, फिर भी 12 फरवरी, 2016 तथा 9 फरवरी, 2016 को मेसर्स ऑलिव ओवरसीज प्रा.लि. तथा नक्षत्र लि., यश वी. जेवेल्स लि. के नाम से चेक निर्गत करते रहे।
- तेजस्वी यादव ने आयकर अधिकारियों को पूछताछ में बताया कि सोने एवं डायमंड की जिन पाँच कंपनियों ने 5 करोड़ ब्याज-मुक्त ऋण के रूप में दिए, उनको वह नहीं जानते हैं। फिर उन कंपनियों के चेक पर उप-मुख्यमंत्री रहते उन्होंने कैसे हस्ताक्षर किए?

सवाल है कि—

- आखिर मुंबई के ज्वेलर्स एवं डायमंड व्यापारियों ने बिना ब्याज के 5 करोड़ रुपयों का कर्जा ए.बी. एक्सपोर्ट्स को क्यों दिया?

नई दिल्ली के पॉश D-1088, न्यू फ्रेंड्स कॉलोनी में बना तेजस्वी यादव का आलीशान मकान

- ए.बी. एक्सपोर्ट्स वर्ष 2007–08 में दिल्ली की पॉश कॉलोनी D-1008 न्यू फ्रेंड्स कॉलोनी की मकान सहित 5 करोड़ रुपए की संपत्ति लालू परिवार को सौंपने के लिए क्यों खरीदी?
- 55 करोड़ रुपए की कीमतवाली इस जमीन पर चार मंजिला मकान (जिसकी निर्माण लागत 60 करोड़ रुपए के करीब होगी) के लिए राशि कहाँ से आई?
- आखिर ए.बी. एक्सपोर्ट्स ने अपने सारे शेयर सहित 115 करोड़ रुपए की जमीन और चार मंजिला मकान लालू परिवार को क्यों सौंप दिया?

□

मिशेल पैकर्स एंड प्रिंटर्स प्रा.लि.

काले धन को ठिकाने लगाने का जरिया

8,000 करोड़ रुपयों के मुखौटा कंपनियों के माध्यम से काले धन को सफेद करने के मामले में जेल में बंद वीरेंद्र जैन/सुरेंद्र जैन का इस्तेमाल लालू परिवार ने चारा घोटाले और रेलमंत्री के नाते अर्जित काले धन को ठिकाने लगाने में किस तरह से किया, इसका खुलासा मिशेल पैकर्स एंड प्रिटर्स प्रा. लि. नामक कंपनी के इस खेल से होता है।

- मात्र 1 लाख रुपए की पूँजी से वर्ष 2002 में लालू प्रसाद की बेटी मीसा भारती द्वारा प्रारंभ मिशेल पैकर्स एंड प्रिंटर्स प्रा.लि. वर्ष 2005-06 में बंद हो गई।
- वर्ष 2005-06 में ही इस कंपनी ने 20 लाख रुपयों में अपनी मशीन को बेच दिया।
- राज्यसभा सांसद और लालू प्रसाद की बेटी मीसा भारती ने अपनी बंद पड़ी कंपनी मिशेल पैकर्स एंड प्रिंटर्स प्रा.लि. के 10 रुपए के शेयर को 100 रुपए में 25 अक्तूबर, 2008 को बेचकर 1 करोड़ 20 लाख रुपए अर्जित किए।
- इन ऊँची कीमतों के शेयर को खरीदनेवाला सुरेंद्र जैन/वीरेंद्र जैन 8,000 करोड़ रुपए के मनी लाउंड्रिंग के मामले में जेल में बंद है।
- इन 100 रुपए के शेयर्स को 11 माह के भीतर ही मीसा भारती ने वापस 10 रुपए में खरीद लिया।
- इस प्रकार, 1 करोड़ 20 लाख रुपए का लालू परिवार का काला धन वीरेंद्र जैन की कंपनी शालिनी होल्डिंग एवं अन्य कंपनियों के माध्यम से सफेद कर लिया गया।
- इन 1 करोड़ 20 लाख रुपए से वर्ष 2008-09 में दिल्ली के सबसे

महँगे इलाके 26, पालम विहार, बिजवासन में एक फार्म हाउस खरीदा गया।

- इस फार्म हाउस की कीमत आज 50 करोड़ रुपए से ज्यादा होगी।

ई.डी. द्वारा जब्त किया गया मीसा भारती का दिल्ली स्थित बिजवासन का फार्म हाउस

मीसा भारती जवाब दें

- बंद पड़ी कंपनी के 10 रुपए के शेयर को कोई कंपनी 100 रुपए में क्यों खरीदेगी ?
- कोई व्यक्ति/कंपनी शेयर को 100 रुपए में खरीदकर एक वर्ष के भीतर 10 रुपए में क्यों बेच देगा ?
- 8,000 करोड़ रुपयों के मनी लाउंड्रिंग के मामले में 21 मार्च, 2017 को गिरफ्तार श्री वीरेंद्र जैन और सुरेंद्र जैन ने ही क्यों इतने शेयर ऊँचे दामों में खरीदकर फिर 10 रुपए में वापस बेच दिए ?
- वर्ष 2008-09 में क्या 1 करोड़ 20 लाख रुपयों का काला धन मुखौटा कंपनी के माध्यम से वैध बनाने का प्रयास नहीं था ?
- वर्ष 2002 में मात्र एक लाख रुपए की पूँजी लगाकर मीसा भारती 50 करोड़ रुपयों की संपत्ति की मालिक बन बैठी।
- रेलमंत्री के नाते लालू प्रसाद को आवंटित 25, तुगलक रोड, नई दिल्ली, आवास का पता मिशेल पैकर्स के लिए इस्तेमाल क्यों किया गया ?
- वर्ष 2008-09 में 48 लाख रुपए का ब्याज-मुक्त कर्ज देनेवालों

का नाम क्यों छिपा लिया गया?

- इस कंपनी के शेयर्स को 8,000 करोड़ रुपयों के मनी लाउंड्रिंग के कारोबारी वीरेंद्र जैन द्वारा 100 रुपए में खरीदना तथा जमीन की खरीद-फरोख्त तब हुई है, जब लालू प्रसाद रेलमंत्री थे। क्या दोनों महज एक संयोग थे?

□

के.एच.के. होल्डिंग प्रा.लि.

मनी लाउंड्रिंग का खेल

प्रेमचंद गुप्ता, ओ.पी. कत्याल, अशोक बंथिया, कांति सिंह, रघुनाथ झा, 8,000 करोड़ रुपए के मनी लाउंड्रिंग के मामले में जेल में बंद वीरेंद्र जैन जैसे लालू परिवार को संपत्ति देनेवाले लोगों की शृंखला में एक और कारोबारी विवेक नागपाल का भी नाम जुड़ गया है।

- विवेक नागपाल ने भी अपनी कंपनी के.एच.के. होल्डिंग प्रा.लि. की दिल्ली की कीमती जमीन लालू परिवार को सौंप दी।
- मीसा भारती ने वर्ष 1998 में स्थापित इस कंपनी को मात्र 1 लाख रुपए में खरीद लिया।
- विवेक नागपाल ने अपने सारे शेयर्स (10 हजार) मीसा भारती को दे दिए।
- आज इस कंपनी में मीसा भारती के 9,900 तथा उनके पति शैलेश कुमार के 100 शेयर्स हैं।
- अन्य कंपनियों के समान इस कंपनी में न कोई कर्मचारी है, न कोई टर्न ओवर है और न ही इसने कोई व्यवसाय किया।
- वर्ष 2011-12 में पहले 42 लाख 33 हजार रुपयों की आवासीय संपत्ति H-27/1, Western Avenue W-8/3 सैनिक फार्म में खरीदी गई।
- फिर अगले साल वर्ष 2012-13 में 1 करोड़ 78 लाख रुपयों से दिल्ली के सबसे महँगे इलाके सैनिक फार्म में 2 बीघा 8 बिस्वा जमीन खरीदी गई।
- कंपनी के रिकॉर्ड के अनुसार, 20 अक्तूबर, 2010 को इस कंपनी को इंडिया बुल्स हाउसिंग फाइनेंस लि. ने 23 करोड़ रुपयों का कर्ज दिया।
- यह कर्ज कब वापस हुआ? वापस भी हुआ या नहीं, यह पता नहीं।
- अक्तूबर 2014 में के.एच.के. होल्डिंग प्रा.लि. के 42 लाख 33 हजार की

आवासीय संपत्ति एवं 1 करोड़ 78 लाख की 2 बीघा 8 बिस्वा जमीन की मालिक लालू की बड़ी बेटी मीसा भारती हो गई।

- आज इस जमीन की कीमत 50 करोड़ रुपए से ज्यादा है।
- मीसा भारती ने इस कंपनी से डायरेक्टर के रूप में वर्ष 2014-15 में वेतन के रूप में 2 लाख 40 हजार रुपए एवं 2015-16 में 1 लाख 20 हजार रुपए प्राप्त किए।

सवाल है कि—

- आखिर विवेक नागपाल ने वर्ष 1998 में स्थापित अपनी कंपनी के.एच.के. होल्डिंग को क्यों लालू परिवार को सौंप दिया?

मीसा भारती का दिल्ली के H-27/1, Western Avenue W-8/3 स्थित सैनिक फार्म, जिसे ई.डी. ने औपबंधिक तौर पर जब्त किया है

- बंद पड़ी कंपनी को इंडिया बुल्स ने 23 करोड़ रुपयों का ऋण क्यों दिया?

- क्या बिना जमीन के मकान खरीदा जाता है? परंतु यहाँ 48 लाख रुपए का मकान वर्ष 2010 में खरीदा गया और फिर वर्ष 2014 में 2 बीघा 8 बिस्वा जमीन 1 करोड़ 78 लाख रुपए में खरीदी गई।
- सरकारी मकान का व्यावसायिक इस्तेमाल नहीं हो सकता है, परंतु के.एच.के. होल्डिंग प्रा. लि. का डायरेक्टर बनने के लिए मीसा भारती एवं उनके पति शैलेश कुमार ने लालू प्रसाद के सरकारी आवास 25, तुगलक रोड, नई दिल्ली के पते का इस्तेमाल क्यों किया?
- आखिर मकान और जमीन खरीदने के लिए बंद पड़ी कंपनी के पास 2 करोड़ 30 लाख रुपए कहाँ से आए?

□

दान के मुखौटे से जमीन/मकान हथियाने का गोरखधंधा

लालू परिवार ने दान के मुखौटे से अकूत बेनामी संपत्ति हासिल की। उन्होंने विधायक, पार्षद, सांसद और मंत्री बनाने के लिए रघुनाथ झा, कांति सिंह, रमा देवी, कुमार राकेश रंजन, मो. शमीम जैसे अनेक नेताओं से जमीन-मकान दान में लिये या कौड़ियों के भाव अपने नाम लिखवा लिये। भ्रष्टाचार से कमाए काले धन को सफेद करने के लिए बी.पी.एल. श्रेणी के ललन चौधरी, रेलवे के खलासी हृदयानंद चौधरी तथा भूमिहीन प्रभुनाथ यादव, चंद्रकांता देवी, सुभाष चौधरी तक से नौकरी, ठेके या अन्य लाभ पहुँचाने के एवज में कीमती जमीन-मकान दान के जरिए हासिल किए गए। ऐसे करीब दस मामले उजागर हुए हैं, जिनमें लालू परिवार ने करोड़ों रुपयों की संपत्ति कौड़ियों के दाम पर राजनेताओं और अपने कारिंदों से दान करवा ली। दरअसल, दान का यह खेल हर काम के लिए रिश्वत लेने तथा काले धन को सफेद करने का एक गोरखधंधा मात्र बन गया था।

□

कांति सिंह ने मंत्री बनने के लिए अपनी संपत्ति लीज पर दी और दान की

लालू प्रसाद ने वर्ष 2004-09 के अपने रेलमंत्रित्व काल में यू.पी.ए. सरकार में मंत्री बनवाने के एवज में रघुनाथ झा के अलावा श्रीमती कांति सिंह से भी राबड़ी देवी के नाम 13 मार्च, 2006 को पटना में 96.2 डिसमिल जमीन 99 साल की लीज पर लिखवा ली। इसके एक साल पहले 6 जनवरी, 2005 को कांति सिंह ने लालू प्रसाद के बेटों तेज प्रताप यादव और तेजस्वी प्रसाद यादव को पटना के चित्तकोहड़ा में 9.39 डिसमिल जमीन और उसमें बना तीन मंजिला मकान मुफ्त में गिफ्ट कर दिया था।

पटना के सगुना, नया टोला स्थित लालू प्रसाद का मकान व खटाल

- श्रीमती कांति सिंह को यू.पी.ए.-1 में श्री लालू प्रसाद ने मानव संसाधन, भारी उद्योग, पर्यटन जैसे विभाग में मंत्री बनवाया था।
- इसके एवज में 13 मार्च, 2006 को श्रीमती कांति सिंह, उनके पति केशव प्रसाद सिंह एवं पुत्र ऋषि कुमार से राबड़ी देवी के नाम 96.2 डिसमिल जमीन 99 साल की लीज पर लिखवा ली गई।
- इस 96.21 डिसमिल जमीन में बाथरूम के साथ तीन कमरे, चहारदीवारी तथा एक नलकूप भी था।
- दानापुर, सगुना की इस करोड़ों की संपत्ति को मात्र 1,250 रुपए प्रति माह के किराए पर 99 साल (2105 तक) की लीज पर राबड़ी देवी ने हासिल कर लिया।
- इस जमीन पर बिजली और पानी के मीटर के साथ-साथ all rents, taxes, rates, cesses, charges, assessments, dues, duties & other outgoing/imposts both present & future may be payable by the lessors. यानी तमाम तरह के शुल्क/करों का भुगतान भी 99 साल तक कांति सिंह ही करती रहेंगी, ऐसा लीज में प्रावधान था।
- जिस 96.21 डिसमिल जमीन को 13 मार्च, 2006 को लीज पर लिया गया था, उसे चार साल बाद 3 अप्रैल, 2010 को बेचा हुआ दिखाया गया है।
- 96.21 डिसमिल जमीन में से 62 डिसमिल जमीन केशव प्रसाद सिंह एवं ऋषि कुमार द्वारा राबड़ी देवी को 3 अप्रैल, 2010 को बेचा हुआ दिखाया गया है, जिस पर 12 फ्लैट्स वाला 'अभ्योदय होम्स' बना हुआ है।
- इसी भूखंड के दूसरे हिस्से 34.21 डिसमिल की बिक्री 29 दिसंबर, 2010 को दिखलाई गई है, जिसमें लालू प्रसाद वर्षों तक खटाल चलाते रहे, जो आज 'लालूजी के खटाल' के नाम से जाना जाता है।
- इस खटाल वाली जमीन के लिए 19.80 लाख रुपए का भुगतान

आवामी को-ऑपरेटिव बैंक के माध्यम से किया गया, जिसके निदेशक 'कबाब मंत्री' के बेटे अरशद अहमद को नोटबंदी के दौरान काले धन को सफेद करने के आरोप में सी.बी.आई. ने गिरफ्तार किया है।

केशव प्रसाद सिंह और ऋषि कुमार से लिखवाई गई 62 डिसमिल जमीन पर बना अभ्योदय होम्स

- इस प्रकार, कांति सिंह की 62 डिसमिल जमीन पर 12 फ्लैट्स 'अभ्योदय होम्स' तथा शेष 34.21 डिसमिल जमीन पर लालू के खटाल की मालकिन श्रीमती राबड़ी देवी बन गईं।

□

कांति सिंह ने तेजस्वी-तेज प्रताप को जमीन-मकान किया गिफ्ट

पटना के चित्तकोहड़ा स्थित कांति सिंह का मकान, जिसके मालिक अब तेज प्रताप और तेजस्वी हैं

लालू प्रसाद मई 2004 में यू.पी.ए.-1 सरकार में रेलमंत्री बने। इसके मात्र सात माह बाद 6 जनवरी, 2005 को श्रीमती कांति सिंह ने तेज प्रताप और तेजस्वी यादव को पटना शहर के चित्तकोहड़ा स्थित अपनी 9.39 डिसमिल जमीन और उसमें बना तीन मंजिला मकान मुफ्त में गिफ्ट कर दिया।

उपर्युक्त 9.39 डिसमिल जमीन मौजा मुजफ्फरपुर, चित्तकोहड़ा, थाना गर्दनीबाग, जिला पटना, तौजी नं.-18215, खाता नं.-113,प्लॉट नं. 1028

स्थित 3 कट्ठा (4,083 वर्ग फीट) जमीन पर पानी व विद्युत् कनेक्शन तथा हर प्रकार की सुविधा से युक्त तीन मंजिला पक्का मकान कांति सिंह ने लालू के नाबालिग लड़कों को दान कर दिया।

दान-पत्र के अनुसार, वर्ष 2005 में जमीन (3 कट्ठा) की कीमत 5 लाख 64 हजार रुपए और भवन निर्माण की लागत 29 लाख 34 हजार रुपए यानी कुल 35 लाख रुपए कीमत दरशाई गई थी।

दान-पत्र में यह भी कहा गया है कि भविष्य में भी कभी कांति सिंह की संतानें इस संपत्ति पर दावा नहीं कर पाएँगी।

आयकर से बचने के लिए जमीन व मकान की कीमत काफी कम दरशाई गई थी, जबकि उस समय भी इसकी कीमत 1 करोड़ रुपए से ज्यादा और वर्तमान में 10 करोड़ रुपए से ज्यादा है।

निबंधन दस्तावेज में मुफ्त में जमीन देने के बारे में लिखा गया है कि 'Donees have been close to the donor like her sons, they have been sincerely serving the donor and have always stood by them like her own sons. The faithful services of donees desired to make a gift in favour of donee.'

यानी 'दान प्राप्त करनेवाले दानकर्ता से लंबे समय से काफी नजदीकी हैं। वे दानकर्ता के पुत्र के समान लंबे समय से हैं। वे निष्ठापूर्वक दानकर्ता की सेवा करते रहे हैं और अपने लड़कों के समान खड़े रहे हैं। उनकी इस विश्वासपूर्वक सेवा से खुश होकर दानकर्ता यह दान कर रहा है।'

सवाल है कि—

- जिस समय गिफ्ट किया गया, उस समय तेज प्रताप और तेजस्वी 15-16 वर्ष के रहे होंगे। 15-16 वर्ष की आयु में तेज प्रताप और तेजस्वी ने कांति सिंह की ऐसी क्या सेवा की, जिससे प्रभावित होकर उन्हें अपनी करोड़ों की संपत्ति दान देनी पड़ी?
- आखिर कांति सिंह ने अपनी करोड़ों की संपत्ति क्यों तेज प्रताप और तेजस्वी को मकान सहित गिफ्ट कर दी? तेज प्रताप तो बाँसुरी बजा

रहे थे और तेजस्वी क्रिकेट खेल रहे थे, तो फिर उन्होंने कांति सिंह की कौन सी सेवा की होगी?

- क्या कांति सिंह यह कहना चाह रही हैं कि उनका बेटा ऋषि नालायक है। उसने सेवा नहीं की, बल्कि राबड़ी देवी के बेटों ने सेवा की?
- क्या टिकट पाने और मंत्री बनने के लिए लालू प्रसाद को करोड़ों रुपयों की रिश्वत दान के जरिए दी गई?

□

रघुनाथ झा ने मंत्री पद की चाहत में करोड़ों की संपत्ति को कर दिया दान

गोपालगंज स्थित स्व. रघुनाथ झा का मकान

चारा घोटाले के आरोप में जब लालू प्रसाद को जेल जाने की नौबत आई, तब जिस रघुनाथ झा ने पूरे बिहार में खून का दरिया बहाने की धमकी दी थी, उन्होंने ही यू.पी.ए.-1 में मंत्री बनने के लिए 18 जून, 2005 को लालू प्रसाद के दो नाबालिग बेटों (तेज प्रताप यादव और तेजस्वी प्रसाद यादव) को गोपालगंज में राष्ट्रीय राजमार्ग-28 से सटी अपनी करोड़ों की संपत्ति महज 8 लाख 75 हजार रुपए कीमत बताकर दान कर दी। तीन कट्ठा 2 धुर और 10 धुरकी राष्ट्रीय मार्ग किनारे की जमीन और उसके 500 वर्ग फीट में सारी सुविधाओं से सुसज्जित तीन मंजिला मकान की कीमत 8 लाख 75 हजार रुपए दिखलाई गई। यह संपत्ति गोपालगंज के मौजा हजियापुर, परगना सिपह, वार्ड नंबर 16, थाना गोपालगंज में स्थित है। दान प्राप्त करनेवालों के नाबालिग होने की स्थिति में राबड़ी देवी ने दस्तावेजों पर हस्ताक्षर किए। दानकर्ता रघुनाथ झा ने भी डीड में दान करने की वजह में दान प्राप्त करनेवाले नाबालिग तेज प्रताप और तेजस्वी द्वारा उनकी सेवा करना बताया है।

सवाल है कि—

- आखिर एक सांसद ने अपनी करोड़ों रुपयों की संपत्ति लालू प्रसाद के दो नाबालिग बेटों को ही क्यों दान कर दी?
- लालू प्रसाद के नाबालिग बेटों ने रघुनाथ झा की ऐसी कौन सी सेवा की, जिससे प्रभावित होकर उन्होंने राष्ट्रीय राजमार्ग के किनारे की अपनी करीब 1 करोड़ रुपए मूल्य की जमीन और मकान को दान में दे दिया?
- क्या यू.पी.ए.-1 में मंत्री बनाने के एवज में रघुनाथ झा को भी अपनी संपत्ति लालू प्रसाद के बेटों को दान करने के लिए मजबूर होना पड़ा?

□

ललन चौधरी : लालू के 'भामाशाह'

राबड़ी देवी को 31 लाख रुपए और हेमा यादव को 62 लाख रुपए की जमीन दान में दी

दानवीर विधान परिषद् कर्मी श्री ललन चौधरी

25 जनवरी, 2014 को विधान परिषद् के चतुर्थ श्रेणी कर्मचारी ललन चौधरी ने 30 लाख 80 हजार रुपए की 1,088.8 वर्गफीट पटना शहर की कीमती जमीन, जिसमें 500 वर्गफीट में बने चहारदीवारी सहित पक्के मकान को श्रीमती राबड़ी देवी को दान कर दिया।

इसके मात्र 18 दिन बाद 13 फरवरी, 2014 को श्री चौधरी ने 62 लाख रुपए की 7.75 डिसमिल जमीन राबड़ी देवी–लालू प्रसाद की पाँचवीं बेटी हेमा यादव को भी दान कर दिया।

राबड़ी देवी को दान में दी गई 16 धुर (1,088.8 वर्गफीट) जमीन (500 वर्गफीट में बने चहारदीवारी सहित मकान) को श्री ललन चौधरी ने 30 मार्च, 2009 को रत्नेश्वर प्रसाद यादव पिता—स्व. ठाकुर प्रसाद यादव, तारपुर, मुंगेर से 3.97 लाख रुपए में खरीदी हुई दिखाई गई है।

हेमा यादव को दान की गई 7.75 डिसमिल जमीन ललन चौधरी ने स्व. देवकी राय के पुत्र विशुनदेव राय से 29 मार्च, 2008 को 4.21 लाख रुपए में खरीदी थी।

राबड़ी देवी को ललन चौधरी द्वारा दान की गई 1,088.8 वर्गफीट जमीन (जिसमें 500 वर्गफीट में चहारदीवारी सहित पक्का मकान बना है) दानापुर, सगुना नया टोला, जिला पटना में खाता संख्या 155, प्लाट नं. 277 है। वहीं हेमा यादव को दान की गई 7.75 डिसमिल जमीन मौजा धनौत, महुआ बाग, थाना दानापुर, जिला पटना, तौजी नं. 5554, थाना नं. 20, खाता नं. 173, सर्वे प्लॉट नं. 1548 में अवस्थित है।

श्री चौधरी ने हेमा यादव तथा राबड़ी देवी को जमीन दान देते समय डीड में लिखा कि 'The Donor (Lalan) is very close to the Donee for a long time & the Donee is also financially helping... desire to make gift his said property.'

सवाल है कि—

- आखिर बी.पी.एल. कार्डधारी गरीब ललन चौधरी के पास जमीन खरीदने के लिए क्रमशः 3 लाख 97 हजार और 4 लाख 21 हजार रुपए कहाँ से आए?
- सियाडीह पंचायत, पो. लकड़ी दरगाह, बड़हरिया, सीवान के रहनेवाले ललन चौधरी को इस दान से क्या फायदा हुआ?

बी.पी.एल. कार्डधारी श्री ललन चौधरी का गाँव स्थित मकान।

- श्रीमती राबड़ी देवी और हेमा यादव ने क्या वित्तीय मदद की, जिसके एवज में श्री चौधरी ने उन दोनों को अपनी 1 करोड़ रुपए की संपत्ति दान में दे दी?
- क्या श्रीमती राबड़ी देवी और लालू प्रसाद ने अपने काले धन का इस्तेमाल कर ललन चौधरी के नाम से जमीन खरीदी तथा फिर पाँच साल बाद दान के माध्यम से अपने और बेटी के नाम से रजिस्ट्री करवाकर वापस ले लिया?
- क्या यह सच नहीं है कि श्री विशुन राय और श्री रत्नेश्वर यादव के परिवार के सदस्यों को रेलवे में नौकरी या अन्य काम के एवज में लालू प्रसाद ने अपने विश्वस्त ललन चौधरी के नाम से वर्ष 2008 और 2009 में पटना शहर की अत्यंत कीमती जमीन मुफ्त में लिखवा ली और छह साल बाद अपनी पत्नी राबड़ी देवी और बेटी

हेमा यादव के नाम से दान करवाकर करोड़ों रुपयों की संपत्ति अपने कब्जे में कर ली।

लालू के खटाल में जानवरों को चारा खिलानेवाले बी.पी.एल. कार्डधारी और विधान परिषद् के कर्मी ललन चौधरी, जिसे राबड़ी देवी के कार्यकाल में विधान परिषद् के तत्कालीन सभापति जाबिर हुसैन ने नियुक्त किया था, दरअसल एक मुखौटा है। केवल लालूजी के काले धन को सफेद करने में ललन चौधरी जैसे लोगों का इस्तेमाल होता रहा है।

□

हृदयानंद चौधरी : रेलवे के खलासी की दानवीरता

हृदयानंद चौधरी

लालू-राबड़ी की बेटी और तेजस्वी यादव की पाँचवीं बहन हेमा यादव को रेलवे के कोचिंग कॉम्पलेक्स स्टोर, राजेंद्र नगर, पटना में कार्यरत खलासी श्री हृदयानंद चौधरी (पिता शंकर चौधरी, ग्राम-इटावा, पोस्ट मीरगंज, थाना उचका गाँव, जिला गोपालगंज) ने भी अपनी पटना शहर स्थित 70 लाख रुपए की 7.76 डिसमिल जमीन दान में दे दी। ललन चौधरी की तरह ही हृदयानंद चौधरी ने भी स्टांप ड्यूटी के तौर पर स्वयं

6 लाख 28 हजार रुपए नकद एस.बी.आई., मुख्य शाखा में जमा कराए।

हृदयानंद चौधरी द्वारा दान में दी गई जमीन का खाता नं.-173, प्लॉट नं.-1548, रकबा-3,375 वर्गफीट (7.75 डिसमिल), जो मौजा-धनौत, महुआ बाग, थाना-दानापुर, जिला-पटना में अवस्थित है।

आश्चर्य है कि—

- सीवान के रहनेवाले ललन चौधरी और गोपालगंज के रहनेवाले हृदयानंद चौधरी ने एक ही दिन 29 मार्च, 2008 को जमीन की खरीद दिखाई।
- जमीन बेचनेवाला एक ही परिवार है। स्व. देवकी राय के पुत्र विशुन राय ने ललन चौधरी को और दूसरे पुत्र ब्रजनंदन राय ने हृदयानंद चौधरी को समान मूल्य 4 लाख 21 हजार रुपयों और समान रकबा 7.75 डिसमिल जमीन बेची।
- क्या यह महज संयोग है कि ललन चौधरी के दान-पत्र पर हृदयानंद चौधरी और हृदयानंद चौधरी के दान-पत्र पर ललन चौधरी गवाह हैं?
- आखिर अलग-अलग जगह के रहनेवाले दोनों दानकर्ताओं—ललन चौधरी और हृदयानंद चौधरी ने लालू प्रसाद की पुत्री श्रीमती हेमा यादव को एक ही दिन 1 करोड़ 40 लाख रुपए की 15 डिसमिल जमीन क्यों दान कर दी?

हेमा यादव को 70 लाख रुपए की जमीन दान करनेवाले हृदयानंद चौधरी की नियुक्ति लालू प्रसाद के रेलमंत्रित्व काल में पूर्व-मध्य रेलवे के ग्रुप डी के पद पर 20 जून, 2005 को हुई थी। ललन चौधरी की तरह ही हृदयानंद चौधरी को नौकरी देने के एवज में उनके नाम से बेनामी संपत्ति लिखवाई गई और फिर गिफ्ट कराकर उसे वापस ले लिया गया। दरअसल, ललन चौधरी और हृदयानंद चौधरी लालू प्रसाद के काले धन और बेनामी संपत्ति को सफेद करने का जरिया मात्र बने।

स्व. देवकी राय
↓ पुत्र

विशुन देव राय
बेचा ↓
ललन चौधरी
सियाढ़ी, बड़हरिया
सीवान

29 मार्च, 2008
7.75 डिसमिल
4.21 लाख रुपए
↓
हेमा यादव
13 फरवरी, 2014
62.10 लाख रुपए
7.75 डिसमिल
6.28 लाख रुपए स्टांप ड्यूटी का
भुगतान ललन चौधरी ने किया।

रत्नेश्वर यादव
S/o स्व. ठाकुर प्रसाद यादव
तारापुर, मुंगेर
बेचा ↓
ललन चौधरी 30 मार्च, 2009
1,088 वर्गफीट (पक्का मकान सहित)
3.97 लाख रुपए
↓
राबड़ी देवी
25 जनवरी, 2014
30.80 लाख रुपए

ब्रजनंदन राय
बेचा ↓
हृदयानंद चौधरी
इटावा, पो. मीरगंज
थाना-उचकागाँव, गोपालगंज

29 मार्च, 2008
7.75 डिसमिल
4.21 लाख रुपए
↓
हेमा यादव
13 फरवरी, 2014
62.10 लाख रुपए
7.75 डिसमिल
6.28 लाख रुपए स्टांप ड्यूटी का
भुगतान हृदयानंद चौधरी ने किया।

प्रभुनाथ यादव : रिश्ते का सौदा

रिश्तेदार के नाम जमीन खरीदकर बेटों के नाम करा लिया दान

- श्री लालू प्रसाद ने नेता प्रतिपक्ष रहते वर्ष 1989 में अपने भूमिहीन व अत्यंत निर्धन साले प्रभुनाथ यादव के नाम पर 2,790 वर्गफीट जमीन मौजा सलेमपुर डुमरा, समनपुरा, थाना शास्त्रीनगर में खरीदी।
- इस जमीन पर लालू प्रसाद के रुपयों से दो मंजिला पक्का मकान बनवाया गया।
- 26 जुलाई, 2006 को श्री प्रभुनाथ यादव ने 2 कट्ठा 1 धुर में बने इस दो मंजिले पक्का मकान (900 वर्गफीट जमीन तल्ले पर और 874 वर्गफीट पहले तल्ले पर) जिसकी कीमत उस समय 14 लाख रुपए दिखाई गई है, श्री तेजस्वी यादव एवं तेज प्रताप यादव को मुफ्त में गिफ्ट कर दिया।
- गिफ्ट डीड में कहा गया है 16–17 वर्ष के तेज प्रताप और तेजस्वी की सेवा से खुश होकर मैं यह कीमती जमीन सहित दो मंजिला मकान गिफ्ट कर रहा हूँ।
- प्रभुनाथ यादव से दान में मिली इस संपत्ति को चार वर्ष बाद 3 अप्रैल, 2010 को तेजस्वी–तेज प्रताप ने अमित कत्याल की कंपनी ए.के. इन्फोसिस्टम्स को 70 लाख रुपयों में बेच दिया।
- मकान सहित 70 लाख रुपयों की जमीन खरीदने के लिए अमित कत्याल ने अपनी दो अन्य कंपनियों फ्रॉस्ट फैलेम डिस्टिलरीज और आइसबर्ग इंडस्ट्रीज से 80 लाख रुपयों का कर्ज ए.के. इन्फोसिस्टम्स को दिलवा दिया, ताकि तेजस्वी की जमीन खरीदी जा सके।
- ए.के. इन्फोसिस्टम्स को 70 लाख रुपयों में जमीन बेचने के चार वर्ष बाद वर्ष 2014 में तेजस्वी और राबड़ी इस कंपनी के सारे शेयर्स 1 लाख रुपए में खरीदकर इस कंपनी के मालिक बन गए।
- इस प्रकार, लालू प्रसाद के रुपयों से प्रभुनाथ के नाम खरीदी गई जमीन

को पहले गिफ्ट करवाया, फिर 70 लाख रुपयों में बेच दिया और फिर कंपनी के माध्यम से उस जमीन के मालिक बन बैठे।

- यानी जमीन बेचकर 70 लाख रुपए कमा लिये और फिर बिना खर्च किए उस जमीन के पुनः मालिक बन बैठे।

सन् 1988 में नेता प्रतिपक्ष रहते प्रभुनाथ
के नाम जमीन लिखवाई।

↓

26 जुलाई, 2006 को अपनी ही जमीन
को प्रभुनाथ से तेज प्रताप-तेजस्वी को गिफ्ट दिखलाया।

↓

3 अप्रैल, 2010 को दान की जमीन को
71 लाख रुपए में ए.के. इन्फोसिस्टम्स को बेचा।

↓

वर्ष 2014 में ए.के. इन्फोसिस्टम्स के मालिक बन गए।

↓

फिर बेची हुई जमीन के मालिक बन गए।

□

सुभाष चौधरी : लालू के पैसों से जमीन खरीद मीसा को किया दान

- लालू प्रसाद के पैसे से (जब वे मुख्यमंत्री थे) श्री सुभाष चंद्र चौधरी सुपुत्र जमादार चौधरी, गोपालगंज के नाम से 4 कट्ठा, 11 धुर जमीन मौजा मैनपुरा, थाना श्रीकृष्णपुरी, पटना के नाम से खरीद दिखलाई गई।
- इस जमीन को नकद भुगतान कर खरीदा गया।
- श्री सुभाष चंद्र चौधरी ने 11 लाख 32 हजार रुपए (वर्ष 2003 का मूल्य) की पटना शहर की अत्यंत कीमती जमीन, जिसकी कीमत आज करोड़ों में होगी, लालू की बेटी मीसा भारती को दान कर दी।
- श्री सुभाष चौधरी की गिफ्ट डीड में लिखा है कि मीसा भारती की सेवा से प्रभावित होकर वह यह जमीन दान कर रहे हैं।
- इस गिफ्ट डीड पर भोला यादव ने गवाह के नाते हस्ताक्षर किए हैं।
- वर्ष 1993 में खरीदी गई जमीन का दस वर्षों तक दाखिल-खारिज नहीं हुआ। जमीन गिफ्ट करने से कुछ माह पूर्व इस जमीन का दाखिल-खारिज सुभाष चौधरी के नाम से कराया गया।
- आखिर गोपालगंज के रहनेवाले सुभाष चंद्र चौधरी को वर्ष 1993 में जमीन खरीदने के लिए किसने पैसा दिया?
- दस वर्षों तक सुभाष चंद्र चौधरी के नाम से जमीन का दाखिल-खारिज क्यों नहीं कराया गया?
- आखिर मीसा भारती ने क्या सेवा की, जिससे प्रसन्न होकर सुभाष चौधरी ने करोड़ों की जमीन उन्हें दान कर दी?
- आखिर सुभाष चंद्र चौधरी ने अपने बच्चों के नाम जमीन लिखने के बजाय मीसा भारती को क्यों गिफ्ट कर दी?

□

चंद्रकांता चौधरी : सास-बहू का दान का रिश्ता

- चंद्रकांता देवी पत्नी राजेश्वर सिंह ग्राम—कुंजवा मनेर, थाना बिहटा, पटना ने भी लालू प्रसाद की बड़ी बेटी मीसा भारती को 318 डिसमिल जमीन दान कर दी।
- मीसा भारती ने दावा किया कि चंद्रकांता देवी पत्नी राजेश्वर सिंह उनकी सास हैं; जबकि मीसा के ससुर रामबाबू पथिक हैं, न कि राजेश्वर सिंह।
- श्रीमती चंद्रकांता देवी ने 8 दिसंबर, 2006 को मौजा—निलाप, मनेर, पटना की 8 लाख, 6 हजार रुपए मूल्य (तत्कालीन मूल्य) की 318 डिसमिल जमीन दान कर दी।
- आश्चर्य है कि गिफ्ट डीड में दान प्राप्तकर्ता के रूप में रोहिणी आचार्य को दिखाया गया है और मीसा भारती के हस्ताक्षर गवाह के नाते हैं।
- परंतु गिफ्ट डीड में फोटो मीसा भारती का लगा हुआ है और नीचे लिखा है—'I have accepted the gift.'—**मीसा भारती**
- आखिर चंद्रकांता देवी ने 318 डिसमिल जमीन मीसा भारती को क्यों दान कर दी?
- आखिर चंद्रकांता देवी ने अपनी संतानों को संपत्ति देने के बजाय मीसा भारती को क्यों दान कर दी?

□

रमा देवी से तेज प्रताप को 3 वर्ष 8 माह की उम्र में 13 एकड़ 12 डिसमिल जमीन मिली दान में

रघुनाथ झा, कांति सिंह, ललन चौधरी, हृदयानंद चौधरी, प्रभुनाथ यादव, सुभाष चौधरी व चंद्रकांता चौधरी की श्रृंखला में बिहार सरकार के तत्कालीन मंत्री स्व. बृजबिहारी प्रसाद की पत्नी श्रीमती रमा देवी ने भी 23 मार्च, 1992 को 13 एकड़ 12 डिसमिल जमीन तेज प्रताप यादव को दान में लिख दी।

- मुजफ्फरपुर जिले के मौजा किशुनपुर मधुबन, थाना—कुढ़नी में एक प्लॉट में 9 एकड़ 24 डिसमिल तथा दूसरे प्लॉट में 3 एकड़ 88 डिसमिल कुल 13 एकड़ 12 डिसमिल जमीन दान की गई।
- गिफ्ट के समय लालू प्रसाद के पुत्र की उम्र 3 वर्ष 8 माह थी।
- दान-पत्र में लिखा गया है कि—
  तेज प्रताप रमा देवी का प्यारा है, जिन्हें रमा देवी बहुत प्यार व मोहब्बत करती हैं और तेज प्रताप भी रमा देवी की खुशी का खयाल रखते हैं। तेज प्रताप नाबालिग हैं; फिर भी, जहाँ तक संभव होता है, रमा देवी की सेवा-शुश्रूषा करते हैं। इससे रमा देवी की इच्छा हुई कि सेवा-शुश्रूषा के कारण अपनी जिंदगी में ही तेज प्रताप को गिफ्ट कर दूँ।
- आखिर 3 साल 8 माह की उम्र में तेज प्रताप ने क्या सेवा की, जिससे खुश होकर यह जमीन दान कर दी गई?
- इस जमीन के नजदीक की सड़क आज भी 'लालू रोड' के नाम से जानी जाती है।

- स्व. बृजबिहारी प्रसाद लालू-राबड़ी सरकार में विज्ञान व प्रौद्योगिकी तथा ऊर्जा विभाग के मंत्री थे।

चौर की सस्ती जमीन पसंद नहीं आई तो दान-पत्र कैंसिल करा दिया

श्रीमती रमा देवी द्वारा गिफ्ट की गई जमीन का मामला उजागर होने के बाद लालू प्रसाद ने उक्त दान-पत्र को कैंसिल कराने का दावा किया। लालू प्रसाद के अनुसार, जून 1993 में गिफ्ट कैंसिल करा दिया गया था। दरअसल, यह गाँव व चौर की सस्ती जमीन थी, जो लालू प्रसाद को पसंद नहीं आई और गिफ्ट लेने के 15 महीने बाद उन्होंने दान-पत्र को कैंसिल कराने का दावा किया।

लालू प्रसाद बताएँ कि—

- जमीन दान की गई मार्च 1992 में और दान-पत्र जून 1993 में कैंसिल कराने का दावा किया गया। आखिर दान-पत्र कैंसिल कराने में 15 महीने क्यों लगे?
- क्या लालू प्रसाद की सहमति के बिना उनके 3 वर्ष 8 माह के पुत्र को दानकर्ता ने जमीन दान कर दी थी?
- क्या चौर की सस्ती जमीन पसंद नहीं आने की वजह से दान-पत्र कैंसिल कराने का दावा किया गया?
- अगर कैंसिल ही करना था तो फिर दान स्वीकार क्यों किया गया?

□

गिफ्ट कैंसिल कराने का दावा

नौ सौ चूहे खा के बिल्ली...

रमा देवी की तरह रघुनाथ, कांति, ललन, हृदयानंद, प्रभुनाथ, सुभाष के गिफ्ट भी कैंसिल कराएँ लालू प्रसाद

अगर लालू प्रसाद को गिफ्ट से परहेज था तो उन्होंने रघुनाथ झा, कांति सिंह, बी.पी.एल. ललन चौधरी, रेलवे के खलासी हृदयानंद चौधरी, भूमिहीन प्रभुनाथ यादव, चंद्रकांता देवी और सुभाष चौधरी से लिये गए गिफ्ट को कैंसिल क्यों नहीं कराया? दरअसल, रमा देवी द्वारा गिफ्ट की गई गाँव व चौर की सस्ती जमीन थी, जो लालू प्रसाद को पसंद नहीं आई और गिफ्ट लेने के 15 महीने बाद उन्होंने दान-पत्र को कैंसिल कराने का दावा किया।

सवाल है कि—

- लालू परिवार ने रघुनाथ झा, कांति सिंह, ललन चौधरी, हृदयानंद चौधरी, प्रभुनाथ यादव, सुभाष चौधरी से मिले दान को आज तक कैंसिल क्यों नहीं कराया?
- श्री रघुनाथ झा ने करोड़ों का तीन मंजिले मकान सहित राष्ट्रीय राजमार्ग के बगल की 3 कट्ठा, 2 धुर व 10 धुरकी जमीन तेज प्रताप और तेजस्वी को वर्ष 2005 में गिफ्ट की। उसे क्यों नहीं आज तक कैंसिल कराया?
- श्रीमती कांति सिंह ने तेज प्रताप और तेजस्वी को पटना में करोड़ों रुपए के मकान सहित 9.39 डिमिल जमीन वर्ष 2005 में दान दी। उसे क्यों नहीं कैंसिल कराया?
- लालू प्रसाद के खटाल में काम करनेवाले श्री ललन चौधरी को लालू ने विधान परिषद् में चपरासी नियुक्त करवाया। उसने राबड़ी

देवी और हेमा यादव को पटना की करोड़ों की जमीन दान की। उसको लालू प्रसाद ने अभी तक कैंसिल क्यों नहीं करवाया?

- लालू प्रसाद के रेलमंत्री रहते खलासी के पद पर नियुक्त हृदयानंद चौधरी द्वारा दान में लिखवाई गई करोड़ों की जमीन को कब कैंसिल कराया जाएगा?
- प्रभुनाथ यादव से तेजस्वी और तेज प्रताप को करोड़ों की जमीन गिफ्ट दिखलाई और उसे ए.के. इन्फोसिस्टम्स को बेच दिया तथा फिर ए.के. इन्फोसिस्टम्स के माध्यम से उसके मालिक बन गए। उस गिफ्ट को आज तक कैंसिल क्यों नहीं किया गया?
- श्री सुभाष चौधरी ने पटना की जो 14 डिसमिल जमीन मीसा भारती को वर्ष 2003 में दान की, उसको आज तक कैंसिल क्यों नहीं किया गया?
- श्री तेजस्वी प्रसाद को वर्ष 2003 में गोपालगंज में मिली 8 कट्ठा 13 धुर दान की जमीन आज तक कैंसिल क्यों नहीं की गई?
- स्व. बृजबिहारी प्रसाद की पत्नी द्वारा 13 एकड़ 13 डिसमिल जमीन तेज प्रताप को 23.03.1992 को दान में दी गई।
- तेज प्रताप को 3 वर्ष 8 माह की उम्र में दान मिला, तब तो लालू प्रसाद ने उसे कैंसिल नहीं कराया। अगर जमीन नहीं मिली तो कैंसिल क्यों कराया?
- अगर इस दान पर लालू प्रसाद की सहमति नहीं थी या दान अधूरा था तो इसे कैंसिल कराने की जरूरत क्या थी?
- फिर दान को कैंसिल कराने में 15 माह क्यों लग गए?
- क्या स्व. बृजबिहारी प्रसाद ने 15 माह तक इसे गुप्त दान रखा?
- क्या दान देनेवाला 15 माह तक छिपाकर रख सकता है?

सच तो यह है कि—

- लालू प्रसाद को चौर की सस्ती जमीन पसंद नहीं आई, इसलिए 15

माह बाद उस दान को रद्द करा दिया। परंतु अन्य शहरों की जमीन अत्यंत कीमती थी, इसलिए आज तक कैंसिल नहीं किया गया।

- लालू प्रसाद में अगर हिम्मत है तो चौर की जमीन के समान अन्य सभी जमीनों का गिफ्ट भी कैंसिल कराएँ।

□

मंगरू यादव को भी नहीं बख्शा

लालू लोगों से बख्शीश लेते रहे
परंतु कभी किसी को बख्शीश नहीं दी

- प्रभावशाली एवं संपन्न लोग दूसरों को दान देते हैं, परंतु लालू परिवार संपन्नता के बावजूद पूरी जिंदगी में किसी गरीब को एक धेला भी दान नहीं किया, बल्कि अपने गरीब रिश्तेदारों के नाम पहले अपना पैसा लगाकर जमीन रजिस्ट्री करवाते रहे और बाद में बेचारों से गिफ्ट करवा लिया।
- अन्यथा स्व. मंगरू यादव के पुत्र क्यों 4 कट्ठा साढ़े 8 धुर दो फसला जमीन खुद खेती करने के बजाय तेज प्रताप को गिफ्ट करते ?
- 1990-96 के दौरान जब लालू यादव बिहार के मुख्यमंत्री थे, उस दौरान उन्होंने अपने बड़े भाई मंगरू यादव के नाम 6 फरवरी, 1992 को 4 कट्ठा साढ़े 8 धुर दो फसला सिंचित जमीन कपिलदेव चौधरी से रजिस्ट्री करवा लिया।
- यह जमीन गोपालगंज जिले के मौजा—फुलवरिया, पंचायत—भागवत परसा, थाना—फुलवरिया के खाता नं.-74, तौजी नं.-3296, सर्वे नं.-892 में अवस्थित है।
- निबंधन दस्तावेज के अनुसार 2003 में इस जमीन की कीमत 44,500 रुपए प्रति कट्ठा की दर से लगभग 2 लाख रुपए थी।
- वर्तमान दर पर इस 4 कट्ठा साढ़े 8 धुर दो फसला सिंचित जमीन की कीमत 40 लाख रुपए के करीब है।
- तेज प्रताप को 15 वर्ष की उम्र में स्व. मंगरू यादव के 4 पुत्रों ने इस कीमती जमीन को बख्शीश (Gift) में दे दिया।

- निबंधन दस्तावेज के अनुसार स्व. मंगरू यादव के 4 पुत्रों—1. रमाशंकर यादव 2. त्रिवेणी यादव, 3. श्यामा यादव, 4. कमल यादव लिखते हैं कि—

"लेख्यधारी (तेज प्रताप) को लेख्यकारीगण के पिता स्व. मंगरू यादव अपने जीवन काल में अपने भतीजा तेज प्रताप यादव बल्द लालू प्रसाद को पुत्र के समान प्यार करते थे तथा उनकी दिली ख्वाहिश हुई कि उक्त जमीन लेख्यधारी (तेज प्रताप) को बख्शीश कर दूँ, लेकिन उनकी आकस्मिक मृत्यु के कारण उनकी दिली ख्वाहिश पूरी नहीं हो पाई। अतएव अपने पिता की दिली ख्वाहिश को पूरा करने के लिए अपने छोटे चचेरे भाई तेज प्रताप यादव से कहे, जिसको तेज प्रताप यादव कबूल कर वह मंजूर करते हुए लिखवाने को तैयार हुए।"

- वास्तविकता यह है कि लालू प्रसाद ने अत्यंत गरीब अपने भाई स्व. मंगरू यादव को मुख्यमंत्री रहते अपना पैसा लगाकर जमीन खरीदवा दिया।
- राबड़ी देवी जब मुख्यमंत्री (2000–05) थी, उस दौरान स्व. मंगरू यादव के बेटों से लाखों की जमीन तेज प्रताप के नाम गिफ्ट करवा दिया।
- 2015 विधानसभा चुनाव के दौरान तेज प्रताप ने नामांकन दाखिल करते समय अपनी संपत्ति घोषणा में इस संपत्ति का उल्लेख नहीं किया था।
- औरंगाबाद की 45 डिसमिल जमीन जिस पर लारा हीरो का शोरूम है, के समान फुलवारिया की इस जमीन को भी चुनाव आयोग से छिपा लिया गया।

□

तीन पीढ़ियों का इंतजाम

एम.एल.सी. बनाने के एवज में 4 प्लॉट का राबड़ी देवी के नाम पॉवर ऑफ एटॉर्नी और तेजस्वी-तेज प्रताप के नाम वसीयत

लालू प्रसाद संपत्ति लिखवाने के लिए नए-नए तरीके ईजाद करते रहे हैं। पॉवर ऑफ एटॉर्नी तथा वसीयत द्वारा भी उन्होंने अपने परिवार के नाम जमीन लिखवाई।

श्री लालू प्रसाद की कृपा से बिहार लोक सेवा आयोग (BPSC) के तत्कालीन चेयरमैन बने श्री रामाश्रय प्रसाद यादव से वर्ष 1994 में मो. शमीम, सोफिया तबस्सुम, राकेश रंजन, सीमा वर्मा ने विजय विहार को-ऑपरेटिव, सगुना, दानापुर में 6,726 वर्गफीट के दो प्लॉट एवं 6,711 वर्ग फीट के दो प्लॉट खरीदे।

मो. शमीम की पत्नी सोफिया तबस्सुम हैं तथा राकेश रंजन की पत्नी सीमा वर्मा हैं।

मो. शमीम को वर्ष 1998 में राज्यपाल कोटे से एम.एल.सी. मनोनीत करवाया गया और राकेश रंजन को वर्ष 1999 से 2006 तक दो बार एम.एल. सी. बनाया गया।

एम.एल.सी. बनने की एवज में मो. शमीम एवं राकेश रंजन ने आपनी और पत्नी के नाम की जमीन सहित 12 मई, 2005 को अपने चारों प्लॉट्स की पॉवर ऑफ एटॉर्नी राबड़ी देवी को दे दी।

पॉवर ऑफ एटॉर्नी के दस्तावेज में लिखा है कि

'राबड़ी देवी उनकी जमीन की देखभाल करेंगी। वे जमीन को किराए पर लगाकर पैसा वसूल सकती हैं। राबड़ी देवी ही मो. शमीम और कुमार राकेश रंजन के बदले कोर्ट में उपस्थित होने तथा मुकदमा लड़ने का काम करेंगी।'

पॉवर ऑफ एटॉर्नी का अर्थ होता है कि जमीन मालिक के बदले जमीन की देखभाल, खरीद-बिक्री राबड़ी देवी कर सकेंगी। जमीन के मालिक मो. शमीम और राकेश रंजन ही बने रहेंगे; परंतु व्यवहार में राबड़ी देवी पॉवर ऑफ एटॉर्नी के माध्यम से जमीन की मालकिन बन बैठी हैं और चुनाव लड़ने के लिए दाखिल दस्तावेज में इस जमीन को अपनी संपत्ति बता रही हैं। इस तरह बिना दाम दिए, बिना रजिस्ट्री कराए पॉवर ऑफ एटॉर्नी के माध्यम से राबड़ी देवी मो. शमीम, सोफिया तबस्सुम, राकेश रंजन, सीमा वर्मा की करोड़ों की जमीन की मालकिन बन बैठी हैं।

जिस पूर्व मुख्यमंत्री की जमीन की देखभाल दूसरे लोग करते हैं, परंतु यहाँ वही पूर्व मुख्यमंत्री दूसरों की जमीन की देखभाल करने का कागजी दावा करती हैं।

फिर उसी दिन (12 मई, 2005 को) इन सबने अलग-अलग उन्हीं जमीनों की वसीयत कर दी कि उनकी मृत्यु के उपरांत इस संपत्ति के मालिक लालू प्रसाद के दोनों पुत्र—तेजस्वी और तेज प्रताप होंगे। वसीयत में यह भी लिखा है कि—"इस संपत्ति पर मेरे किसी वैधानिक उत्तराधिकारी या अन्य किसी का कोई कानूनी अधिकार नहीं होगा।''यदि तेजस्वी या तेज प्रताप की मृत्यु हो जाती है तो उनके 'वैधानिक उत्तराधिकारी' इसके मालिक होंगे।"

मो. शमीम और कुमार राकेश रंजन से उन्हें एम.एल.सी. बनाने की पूरी कीमत लालू प्रसाद ने पहले चार प्लॉट्स की राबड़ी देवी के नाम पॉवर ऑफ एटॉर्नी और फिर तेजस्वी और तेज प्रताप के नाम से वसीयत कराकर वसूल ली।

क्या यह महज संयोग है कि—

- मो. शमीम और कुमार राकेश रंजन ने स्वयं और अपनी पत्नी के नाम से एक ही वर्ष 1994 में एक ही परिवार डॉ. रामाश्रय यादव से जमीन लिखवाई ?
- मो. शमीम और राकेश रंजन दोनों को लालू प्रसाद ने एम.एल.सी. बनाया।

एम.एल.सी. बनने के लिए मो. शमीम और कुमार राकेश रंजन द्वारा दी गई सगुना-खगौल रोड से सटे विजय विहार को-ऑपरेटिव स्थित भूखंड

- मो. शमीम और राकेश रंजन ने एक ही दिन स्वयं और पत्नी के चार प्लॉट्स की पॉवर ऑफ एटॉर्नी राबड़ी देवी को दे दी।
- पॉवर ऑफ एटॉर्नी का मतलब जमीन मालिक के बदले जमीन की देखभाल करना होता है; परंतु राबड़ी देवी उन चारों प्लॉट्स को अब अपनी संपत्ति बता रही हैं और उसे अपने चुनाव आयोग के डिक्लेरेशन में शामिल कर रखा है।
- कुमार राकेश रंजन और मो. शमीम ने अपने और पत्नी के चार प्लॉट्स की वसीयत एक ही दिन तेजस्वी और तेज प्रताप के नाम कर दी।

- मो. शमीम के दस्तावेज पर कुमार राकेश रंजन और कुमार राकेश रंजन के दस्तावेज पर मो. शमीम गवाह हैं।

सवाल है कि—

- क्या एक पूर्व मुख्यमंत्री (श्रीमती राबड़ी देवी) को इतनी फुरसत है कि पॉवर ऑफ एटॉर्नी लेकर दूसरों की जमीन की देखभाल करें?
- मो. शमीम और राकेश रंजन की लालू परिवार से कोई रिश्तेदारी नहीं है। फिर उन लोगों ने क्यों अपनी जमीन पहले पॉवर ऑफ एटॉर्नी और फिर वसीयत के जरिए उनके परिवार को दे दी?
- आखिर क्यों कुमार राकेश रंजन और सीमा वर्मा तथा मो. शमीम और सोफिया तबस्सुम अपनी संतानों के होते हुए पटना शहर के अपने दो-दो कीमती प्लॉट्स की वसीयत तेजस्वी और तेज प्रताप को कर दी?
- आखिर तेजस्वी और तेज प्रताप ने 15 साल की उम्र में मो. शमीम और कुमार राकेश रंजन दंपती की ऐसी क्या सेवा की और उनके पिता लालू प्रसाद ने क्या मदद की, जिससे प्रसन्न होकर दोनों परिवारों ने अपनी करोड़ों की संपत्ति तेजस्वी और तेज प्रताप के नाम वसीयत कर दी?
- आखिर क्यों कुमार राकेश रंजन और मो. शमीम ने लालू प्रसाद की तीन पीढ़ियों के लिए संपत्ति का इंतजाम कर दिया? पहले राबड़ी देवी, फिर तेजस्वी व तेज प्रताप और फिर उनकी भी संतानों को संपत्ति का मालिक बना दिया?

□

सुभाष चंद्र चौधरी ने भी पावर ऑफ एटॉर्नी के माध्यम से राबड़ी को सौंप दी जमीन

- पहले सुभाष चंद्र चौधरी ने पटना की करोड़ों की जमीन मीसा भारती को गिफ्ट कर दिया, फिर गोपालगंज की 2 कट्ठा जमीन राबड़ी देवी को पावर ऑफ एटॉर्नी द्वारा जिंदगी भर के लिए सौंप दिया।
- श्री सुभाष चंद्र चौधरी पिता-जमादार चौधरी, ग्राम—ऊँचका गाँव, टोला—नरगछिया, परगना—कुआरी, जिला गोपालगंज के नाम से 2002 में उपरोक्त जमीन की खरीद दिखलाई गई।
- यह 2 कट्ठा जमीन मौजा—अमरखेम, थाना—मीरगंज, खाता न.-121, तौजी न.-3296 में अवस्थित है।
- इस जमीन को 2002 में जब राबड़ी देवी मुख्यमंत्री थीं, उस समय यह खरीद नकद से दिखलाई गई है।
- खरीद के मात्र 3 साल के भीतर 19 सितंबर, 2005 को सुभाष चंद्र चौधरी ने यह कीमती जमीन पावर ऑफ एटॉर्नी के माध्यम से राबड़ी देवी को सौंप दी।

प्रश्न यह है कि—

- आखिर सुभाष चंद्र चौधरी ने पटना की कीमती जमीन अपने बच्चों को लिखने के बजाय मीसा भारती को क्यों लिख दिया?
- उसी सुभाष चंद्र चौधरी ने गोपालगंज की 2 कट्ठा जमीन पावर ऑफ एटॉर्नी के माध्यम से राबड़ी देवी को सौंप दिया।
- वास्तविकता तो यह है कि लालू परिवार अपने कालेधन का इस्तेमाल कर सुभाष चंद्र चौधरी के नाम से जमीन की खरीद दिखला दिया।

- फिर कुछ वर्षों के बाद उसी जमीन को पावर ऑफ एटॉर्नी के माध्यम से राबड़ी देवी को सौंप दिया।
- राबड़ी देवी द्वारा चुनाव आयोग को सौंपे गए शपथ-पत्र में इस जमीन का कहीं भी उल्लेख नहीं है।

□

लीज द्वारा 255 डिसमिल जमीन के मालिक बने तेजस्वी यादव

गिफ्ट, बेनामी कंपनी, पॉवर ऑफ अटॉर्नी, वसीयत की कड़ी में लीज द्वारा भी जमीन पर कब्जा करने का नायाब तरीका लालू परिवार ने खोज निकाला है। पहले गरीब रिश्तेदारों के नाम से अपना पैसा लगाकर जमीन रजिस्ट्री कराओ और फिर आजीवन लीज के माध्यम से उस जमीन को अपने कब्जे में ले लो।

- पटना सिटी अनुमंडल के रानीपुर खिड़की, मिर्चाइ रोड, पटना की 255 डिसमिल जमीन, जिसकी कीमत करोड़ों में है, के भी मालिक तेजस्वी प्रसाद यादव बन गए हैं।
- इस 255 डिसमिल जमीन को लालू-राबड़ी ने अपने मुख्यमंत्रित्व काल 1990-2005 के बीच अपने बड़े भाई (लालूजी के बड़े भाई) स्व. मुकुंद प्रसाद, जो वेटनरी कॉलेज में चतुर्थ वर्गीय कर्मचारी थे, के समधियाने में अलग-अलग नाम से अपना पैसा लगाकर खरीदवा दिया।
- वर्ष 1991, 2004, 2010, 2012 में कुल छह डीड के माध्यम से 104.32 डिसमिल जमीन खरीदी गई।
- इसी प्रकार रजनीकांत सिंह के भाई शशिकांत सिंह, रविकांत सिंह एवं रजनीकांत की माँ उमा देवी के नाम चार अलग-अलग डीड के माध्यम से 95.23 डिसमिल जमीन खरीदी गई।
- रजनीकांत के मामा शिव कुमार सिंह और राम कुमार सिंह पिता—स्व. सीताराम सिंह, ग्राम—आलमपुर, पी.एस.—दीदारगंज, पी.ओ.—कच्ची दरगाह, पटना के नाम से भी 55.66 डिसमिल जमीन वर्ष

1991 में खरीदी गई।

- यह कुल 255.21 डिसमिल जमीन रानीपुर खिड़की, मिर्चाइ रोड, टेंट सिटी, पटना सिटी को 91 साल के लीज पर श्री तेजस्वी यादव ने लिखवा लिया।
- 13 जून, 2012 को श्री तेजस्वी प्रसाद यादव ने श्री शिव कुमार सिंह (27.66 डि.), 2. राम कुमार सिंह (28 डि.), 3. रजनीकांत सिंह (104.32 डि.), 4. शशिकांत सिंह (39.91 डि.), 5. रविकांत सिंह (27.66 डि.), 6. उमा देवी (27.66 डि.) से कुल 255.21 डि. जमीन 91 साल के लीज पर लिखवा लिया।
- 255.21 डिसमिल जमीन पर 91 वर्ष, यानी 1 जून, 2012 से 31 मई, 2101 तक तेजस्वी प्रसाद यादव का कब्जा बना रहेगा।
- यानी तेजस्वी 110 वर्ष की आयु तक इस जमीन के मालिक बने रहेंगे।
- 55.66 डि. जमीन का वार्षिक किराया मात्र 5 हजार रुपए तथा 199.55 डि. जमीन मात्र 15 हजार वार्षिक किराए पर तेजस्वी ने अपने नाम लिखवा लिया।
- यानी मात्र 20 हजार रुपए प्रति वर्ष किराए पर 91 साल तक (यानी 110 वर्ष की उम्र तक) तेजस्वी इस जमीन के मालिक बने रहेंगे।
- 91 साल के बाद यदि लीज का नवीनीकरण नहीं हो पाया तो 1 हजार रुपए प्रति माह की दर से मुआवजा दिया जाएगा और नवीनीकरण तेजस्वी की मरजी पर निर्भर करेगा।
- आज उस इलाके में जमीन का किराया 5 रुपए प्रति वर्ग फीट है, यानी 255.21 डिसमिल जमीन=1,10,925 वर्ग फीट होता है। 5 रुपए की दर से यह किराया 5,54,625 रुपए प्रति वर्ष होना चाहिए; परंतु निर्धारित करवा लिया मात्र 20 हजार रुपए प्रति वर्ष।
- जमीन का मूल्य लगातार बढ़ता रहता है। परंतु बाजार मूल्य कुछ भी हो तेजस्वी यादव 91 साल तक 20 हजार रुपए ही किराया देते रहेंगे।

- इस लीज एग्रीमेंट में महँगाई के अनुसार लीज दर में वृद्धि का भी कोई प्रावधान नहीं है।
- साधारणतया लीज एग्रीमेंट 30 साल से ज्यादा का नहीं होता है तथा कुछ वर्षों के बाद 10–15 प्रतिशत वृद्धि का भी प्रावधान रहता है।
- परंतु तेजस्वी के लीज एग्रीमेंट में जिंदगी भर 20 हजार रुपए प्रति वर्ष किराए का ही प्रावधान है।
- आज उस इलाके में 25–30 लाख रुपए प्रति कट्ठा जमीन का मूल्य है; परंतु तेजस्वी करोड़ों रुपए की जमीन के आजीवन मालिक मात्र 20 हजार रुपए वार्षिक किराया देकर बन गए हैं।

प्रश्न है कि—

- जो 16 डि. जमीन रजनीकांत सिंह के नाम 31 मार्च, 2012 को 5 लाख 12 हजार में नकद खरीद दिखलाई गई, उसे मात्र 3 माह बाद 91 साल के लीज पर दिखलाई गई।
- आखिर कोई व्यक्ति क्यों पहले लाखों रुपए लगाकर जमीन खरीदेगा और फिर तीन महीने में कौड़ी के भाव जिंदगी भर के लिए लीज पर दे देगा?
- वास्तविकता यह है कि अपने काले धन का इस्तेमाल कर पहले अलग-अलग रिश्तेदारों के नाम जमीन रजिस्ट्री कराई गई और फिर 91 साल का लीज मात्र 15 हजार रुपए वार्षिक किराए पर लेकर तीन पीढ़ी के लिए उस जमीन के मालिक बन गए।
- यदि जमीन अपने नाम रजिस्ट्री कराते तो इतना पैसा आय कर विभाग को कैसे दिखलाते?
- इसलिए लीज के माध्यम से जमीन का मालिक बनने का एक और नया तरीका ईजाद किया गया।

□

तेजस्वी केवल 750 करोड़ रुपए का मॉल ही नहीं बनवा रहे थे, बल्कि करोड़ों के लोहे का व्यापार भी करते हैं

तेजस्वी यादव केवल 750 करोड़ रुपए का मॉल ही नहीं बनवा रहे थे, बल्कि लारा एंड संस नामक लोहा एवं स्टील बेचनेवाले प्रतिष्ठान के भी मालिक हैं। तेजस्वी यादव जिंदल स्टील एंड पॉवर लि., जिंदल सेंटर,12 भीकाजी कामा प्लेस, नई दिल्ली के हैंडलिंग व स्टोरेज एजेंट के रूप में वर्ष 2012 से काम कर रहे हैं।

तेजस्वी यादव का पटना सिटी के रानीपुर खिड़की, मिर्चाइ रोड स्थित स्टॉकयार्ड में खड़ी क्रेन, जहाँ से जिंदल स्टील के हैंडलिंग व स्टोरेज का कारोबार किया जाता है

- जिंदल स्टील ने तेजस्वी यादव को 28 सितंबर, 2012 को रामगढ़, पतरातू Argul के स्टील प्लांट से निर्मित माल हेतु हैंडलिंग व स्टोरेज एजेंट नियुक्त किया।

- श्री तेजस्वी यादव ने लारा एंड संस रानीपुर खिड़की, मिर्चाइ रोड, पटना सिटी के नाम से लोहा व स्टील का व्यापार करने के लिए VAT का रजिस्ट्रेशन नं. TIN-1006226406२ वाणिज्य कर विभाग के पूर्वी अंचल से प्राप्त किया।
- इसके अतिरिक्त Central Sales Tax (CST) तथा Entry Tax का रजिस्ट्रेशन भी प्राप्त किया गया।
- इस व्यापार को करने के लिए भारतीय स्टेट बैंक खाता सं.-30295914683, PAN-ACSPY9993J, मो.नं.-9473240226 का इस्तेमाल किया गया।

हैंडलिंग एजेंट हेतु निम्न शर्तें लगाई गईं—

- रेलवे वैगन से आनेवाले लोहे को प्राप्त करना।
- रेलवे से माल छुड़ाकर उपयुक्त क्रेन द्वारा स्टॉक यार्ड में वे ब्रिज (weigh bridge) पर तौलकर व्यवस्थित तरीके से लोहे को रखना।
- स्टॉक यार्ड पूरी तरह से चहारदीवारी से घिरा हो, सेक्युरिटी गार्ड तथा एस्बेटस एवं तारपोलिन से सुरक्षित होना चाहिए।
- इस पूरे काम के लिए सड़क मार्ग से लोहा आने पर 500 रुपए प्रति टन तथा रेल मार्ग से आने पर 700 रुपए टन हैंडलिंग चार्ज दिया जाएगा।
- इस JSPL स्टॉक यार्ड एग्रीमेंट पर जिंदल स्टील के अधिकृत प्रतिनिधि के तौर से श्रीमती रूपाली मेहरा, पुत्री सुश्री एन.के. शर्मा तथा लारा एंड संस के मालिक के रूप में तेजस्वी प्रसाद यादव ने हस्ताक्षर किए।
- सहमति-पत्र पर हस्ताक्षर करते समय यह भी कहा गया कि श्री तेजस्वी यादव के पास लोहा व स्टील के हैंडलिंग का पर्याप्त अनुभव एवं आवश्यक संरचना है।
- इस सहमति-पत्र पर श्री भोला यादव ने गवाह के रूप में हस्ताक्षर किया।

- इस व्यापार को करने के लिए 255 डिसमिल जमीन पर 12 फीट से ज्यादा ऊँची चहारदीवारी का निर्माण किया गया, जिस पर करोड़ों रुपए खर्च हुए।
- अभी भी इस परिसर में क्रेन, लोहा व स्टील तथा अन्य उपयोगी सामान रखे हुए हैं।
- कुछ माह पूर्व तक इस चहारदीवारी-युक्त जमीन पर लारा एंड संस का बोर्ड लगा हुआ था।
- अभी भी चहारदीवारी पर जिंदल कंपनी का वॉल पेंटिंग किया हुआ है।

प्रश्न यह है कि—

- जिंदल कंपनी के लोहा व स्टील के हैंडलिंग एजेंट के तथ्यों को आज तक छुपाया क्यों गया?
- चुनाव आयोग को दिए गए संपत्ति के ब्योरे में इस जमीन तथा व्यापार का उल्लेख क्यों नहीं किया गया?
- श्री तेजस्वी यादव जिंदल कंपनी के एजेंट के रूप में करोड़ों का व्यापार करते रहे, परंतु VAT के रिटर्न में टर्नओवर शून्य दिखाते रहे।
- आखिर तेजस्वी यादव 22 वर्ष की उम्र में डिलाइट मार्केटिंग, ए.बी. एक्सपोर्ट, लारा एंड संस, फेयर ग्रो जैसी कंपनियों के मालिक कैसे बन गए?

□

29 साल की उम्र में तेजस्वी यादव 5 मकान, 47 जमीन सहित कुल 52 संपत्ति के मालिक

तेजस्वी यादव के खिलाफ बेनामी संपत्ति के आरोप में सी.बी.आई. ने जब एफ.आई.आर. दर्ज की, ई.डी. और आई.टी. ने शिकंजा कसा तो बचने के लिए कहते हैं कि ये सारी संपत्ति तो तब की है, जब वह निमूछा यानी नाबालिग थे। हकीकत है कि कुल 52 संपत्तियों में से 14 के मालिक वे तब बने, जब वे या तो दुधमुँहे बच्चे थे या कक्षा 8-9 में पढ़ाई कर रहे थे। 23 संपत्तियों के मालिक उस समय बने, जब वे 24 वर्ष की उम्र के थे, यानी दाढ़ी-मूँछ थी और पूर्णतया बालिग थे। उनकी कुल 52 में से 23 संपत्तियों को आय कर विभाग/सी.बी.आई. ने बेनामी घोषित कर औपबंधिक रूप से जब्त कर लिया है।

सच तो यह है कि बिहार के सबसे बड़े मॉल के निर्माण का एग्रीमेंट 5 मई, 2016 को सुरसंड के राजद विधायक अबू दोजाना की कंपनी के साथ जब किया गया, तब तेजस्वी यादव केवल दाढ़ी-मूँछवाले ही नहीं, बल्कि राज्य सरकार के उपमुख्यमंत्री भी थे।

हकीकत है कि—

- तेजस्वी प्रसाद यादव एवं सात अन्य पर सी.बी.आई. ने Criminal conspiracy, Cheating & Criminal misconduct का एफ.आई.आर. IPC की धारा 120 B r/w 420 तथा Prevention of Corruption Act.,1988 की धारा 13(2) r/w13(1)(d) के तहत दर्ज किया है।
- एफ.आई.आर. में कहा गया है कि—

वर्ष 2010 से 2014 के बीच प्रेमचंद गुप्ता की पत्नी सरला गुप्ता ने डिलाइट मार्केटिंग कंपनी को श्रीमती राबड़ी देवी एवं तेजस्वी यादव को स्थानांतरित कर दिया, यानी जिस समय तेजस्वी यादव कंपनी के मालिक बने, वह बालिग थे। उनकी दाढ़ी-मूँछ थी। वे निमुछा नहीं थे, जैसा वह दावा करते हैं।

- एफ.आई.आर. में यह भी कहा गया है कि वर्ष 2014 (जब तेजस्वी 24 वर्ष के थे) में जब डिलाइट मार्केटिंग के शेयर पूरी तरह से तेजस्वी को ट्रांसफर किए गए, उस समय बाजार दर 94 करोड़ रुपए तथा सर्किल रेट 32.5 करोड़ रुपयों की जमीन को मात्र 65 लाख रुपए में कब्जे में ले लिया गया।
- जब तेजस्वी यादव नाबालिग थे (16 वर्ष), तब उन्हें कांति सिंह, रघुनाथ झा और प्रभुनाथ यादव की करोड़ों रुपयों की जमीन सहित मकान दान में स्वीकार करने में कोई हिचक नहीं हुई।
- तेजस्वी यादव के नाम गोपालगंज और पटना में कुल 14 भूखंड रजिस्टर्ड हैं। ये सभी संपत्तियाँ उस समय रजिस्ट्री कराई गईं, जब वह नाबालिग थे।
- दो संपत्तियों की तब रजिस्ट्री हुई, जब वह मात्र तीन वर्ष के थे।
- तेजस्वी यादव के नाम बाकी अचल संपत्तियों की रजिस्ट्री उस अवधि में हुई, जब वे नाबालिग थे और उनके पिता यू.पी.ए. सरकार में रेलमंत्री थे।
- यानी नाबालिग (निमूछा) रहते उन्होंने इतनी संपत्ति इकट्ठा कर ली, लेकिन उस समय उन्होंने कभी संपत्ति लेने से इनकार नहीं किया।
- डिलाइट मार्केटिंग की 3.5 एकड़ जमीन जब सरला गुप्ता ने तेजस्वी को वर्ष 2013-14 में सौंपी, उस समय वे दाढ़ी-मूँछ सहित पूर्ण बालिग थे।
- जब तेजस्वी ने 3.5 एकड़ जमीन पर 7 लाख 66 हजार वर्ग फीट के 12 मंजिले मॉल के निर्माण का एग्रीमेंट 5 मई, 2016 को सुरसंड के विधायक अबू दोजाना की कंपनी के साथ किया, उस समय वह केवल

दाढ़ी-मूँछ वाले ही नहीं, बल्कि राज्य सरकार के उपमुख्यमंत्री भी थे।

- डिलाइट मार्केटिंग, ए.बी. एक्सपोर्ट्स, ए.के. इन्फोसिस्टम्स, फेयर ग्रो के माध्यम से जब तेजस्वी दिल्ली एवं पटना की 23 अन्य संपत्तियों (मकान सहित) के मालिक बने, उस समय वह दुधमुँहे बच्चे नहीं, बल्कि 23 वर्ष के पूर्ण बालिग थे।
- इस प्रकार तेजस्वी यादव 5 मकान एवं 47 भूखंड सहित कुल 52 सम्पत्ति के मालिक हैं जिनमें 23 भूखंड खोखा कंपनियों के मध्यम से, 5 भूखंड लीज एवं चार भूखंड वसीयत तथा 14 भूखंड रजिस्ट्री के माध्यम से हासिल किया गया है।
- इसी प्रकार तेजस्वी यादव रघुनाथ झा से गोपालगंज में एक दो मंजिला मकान, श्रीमती कांति सिंह व प्रभुनाथ यादव से पटना में एक-एक दो मंजिला मकान दान करवा लिए। वहीं, ए.बी. एक्सपोर्ट्स के माध्यम से दिल्ली में एक चार मंजिला मकान एवं फेयर ग्रो के जरिए पटना में टिस्को का दो मंजिला मकान हासिल कर लिया।
- राबड़ी देवी के मुख्यमंत्रित्व काल में बिहटा में शराब की फैक्टरी लगानेवाले Iceberg Industries के मालिक अमित काल्याल ने तेजस्वी को 30.26 लाख रुपए एवं एक अन्य कंपनी Triangle Trading Ltd. द्वारा 2010 में 9.5 लाख की गाड़ी उपलब्ध कराई। कर्ज दिए गए 30.26 लाख बाद में अमित कत्याल द्वारा Write off कर दिए गए।
- गिफ्ट लेते समय या जमीन लिखवाते समय उन्होंने कभी नहीं कहा कि मुझे दाढ़ी-मूँछ नहीं है, इसलिए जमीन नहीं लूँगा; परंतु दाढ़ी-मूँछ होने पर बेनामी संपत्तियों के मालिक बन गए। जब जाँच में फँस गए तो कहते हैं कि मुझे तो उस समय दाढ़ी-मूँछ भी नहीं थी।

□

पेट्रोल पंप का मालिक लालू परिवार

दूसरे की जमीन को अपनी बताकर लिया आवंटन

तेज प्रताप का पेट्रोल पंप घोटाला

बिहार के पूर्व स्वास्थ्य मंत्री तेज प्रताप यादव ने पटना के न्यू बाईपास पर बेऊर इलाके में गलत कागजात के आधार पर दूसरे के नाम की जमीन अपनी बताकर अधिकारियों की मिलीभगत से वर्ष 2011 में भारत पेट्रोलियम का एक पेट्रोल पंप अपने नाम आवंटित करा लिया था। धोखाधड़ी कर हासिल किए गए भारत पेट्रोलियम के पेट्रोल पंप के आवंटन को 20 जुलाई, 2017 को कोर्ट के आदेश के बाद रद्द कर दिया गया।

भारत पेट्रोलियम के पेट्रोल पंप रद्द करने के आदेश पर पटना के सब जज–11 श्रीमती शची मिश्रा की अदालत ने पिछले दिनों स्टे लगा दिया था। सब जज–11 की अदालत द्वारा 20 जुलाई को स्टे ऑर्डर वापस लेने के बाद उसी दिन देर रात भारत पेट्रोलियम ने अपने कब्जे में लेकर पेट्रोल पंप को सील कर दिया।

तेज प्रताप यादव पर तथ्यात्मक आरोप है कि जिस समय वर्ष 2011 में उन्होंने पेट्रोल पंप की अनुज्ञप्ति के लिए आवेदन दिया और साक्षात्कार में शामिल हुए, उस समय एन.एच.–30 न्यू बाईपास की 43 डिसमिल जमीन उनके पास नहीं थी।

बिहटा में बीयर फैक्टरी लगानेवाले अमित कत्याल ने 9 जनवरी, 2012 को ए.के. इन्फोसिस्टम्स के एम.डी. के नाते तेजस्वी यादव को पेट्रोल पंप लगाने के लिए 136 डिसमिल जमीन लीज पर दे दी। पेट्रोल पंप के लिए आवेदन दिया तेज प्रताप यादव ने, परंतु जमीन लीज पर पेट्रोल पंप के लिए मिली तेजस्वी यादव को।

गलत कागजात के आधार पर हासिल तेज प्रताप यादव के पेट्रोल पंप का आवंटन बाद में भारत पेट्रोलियम ने रद्द कर दिया।

जब तेज प्रताप यादव की न तो अपनी जमीन थी और न ही लीज उनके नाम से थी तो फिर यह पेट्रोल पंप कैसे आवंटित किया गया?

सवाल है कि—

- वर्ष 2011 में पेट्रोल पंप के लिए आवेदन एवं साक्षात्कार के समय जब तेज प्रताप के नाम से कोई जमीन नहीं थी तो फिर किस आधार पर आवेदन किया गया?
- पेट्रोल पंप आवंटित हुआ तेज प्रताप यादव के नाम से, परंतु पेट्रोल पंप लगाने के लिए ए.के. इन्फोसिस्टम ने तेजस्वी यादव के नाम से वर्ष 2012 में 136 डिसमिल जमीन लीज क्यों किया?
- आखिर वर्ष 2014 में बिहटा में बीयर फैक्टरी लगानेवाले अमित

कत्याल ने अपनी कंपनी ए.के. इन्फोसिस्टम्स और पटना शहर की करोड़ों की जमीन लालू परिवार को क्यों सौंप दी?

□

लारा इंटीरियर्स प्रा.लि.–‘ला’ से लालू, ‘रा’ से राबड़ी

- 17 जनवरी, 2005 को लारा इंटीरियर्स प्रा.लि., ऑफिस : एफ-8 पटना सुपर मार्केट, फ्रेजर रोड, पटना के नाम से एक कंपनी गठित की गई।

- 22 मार्च, 2010 को इस कंपनी का नाम बदलकर लारा डिस्ट्रिब्यूटर्स प्रा.लि. 208, कौटिल्य नगर, पटना कर दिया गया।
- डॉ. मीसा भारती, चंदा यादव, राबड़ी देवी, रागिनी लालू इस कंपनी के डायरेक्टर नियुक्त किए गए। श्री तेज प्रताप यादव 21 अप्रैल, 2010 को एम.डी. नियुक्त किए गए और इस कंपनी में अभी भी 2 लाख 51 हजार शेयर्स के हिस्सेदार हैं।
- इसके अतिरिक्त मीसा भारती (1,000) चंदा यादव (2,000), राबड़ी देवी, (1 लाख 17 हजार) और रागिनी (1 लाख) शेयर के हिस्सेदार हैं।
- श्री तेज प्रताप यादव 16 जनवरी, 2010 को मौजा शाहपुर टोले (कामा बिगहा) थाना न. 561, तौजी 4967, थाना औरंगाबाद, जिला औरंगाबाद, नगर परिषद् क्षेत्र औरंगाबाद के वार्ड न. 26 में सीता देवी, बिनेश्वर साव, फूलमती देवी, सरस्वती देवी, जिलाल यादव एवं अनिता कुमारी (इनके नाम से दो डीड हैं) से 53 लाख 34 हजार रुपए में 45.24 डिसमिल जमीन खरीदी और अपने नाम से रजिस्ट्री कराई।
- इसी जमीन पर हीरो होंडा मोटरसाइकिल का तीन मंजिला शोरूम एन.एच. के बगल में मुख्य सड़क पर अवस्थित है।
- 2 फरवरी, 2012 को इस जमीन को गिरवी रखकर मध्य बिहार ग्रामीण बैंक, औरंगाबाद से 2 करोड़ 29 लाख रुपयों का कर्ज प्राप्त किया गया।
- वर्ष 2015 के विधानसभा चुनाव के समय चुनाव आयोग तथा बिहार सरकार के समक्ष संपत्ति का ब्योरा देते समय इस संपत्ति के ब्योरे को छिपा लिया गया।
- उपर्युक्त संपत्ति को गिरवी रखकर 2 करोड़ 29 लाख रुपयों के कर्ज को भी चुनाव आयोग तथा बिहार सरकार में घोषित संपत्ति के ब्योरे में छिपा लिया गया।

सवाल है कि—

- वर्ष 2010 में 20 वर्ष की आयु में 45.24 डिसमिल जमीन खरीदने के लिए 53 लाख 34 हजार रुपए कहाँ से आए?
- इस जमीन की खरीद लारा डिस्ट्रिब्यूटर्स के नाम से नहीं, बल्कि व्यक्तिगत तेज प्रताप यादव के नाम से की गई थी।
- इस 45.24 डिसमिल जमीन (जिसकी कीमत आज 15 करोड़ रुपयों से कम नहीं होगी) को क्यों चुनाव आयोग एवं राज्य सरकार से छिपा लिया गया?
- इस जमीन पर 2 करोड़ 29 लाख रुपयों का कर्ज है, इसे क्यों छिपा लिया गया?

जान-बूझकर आपराधिक कृत्य : तेज प्रताप ने छुपाई औरंगाबाद की संपत्ति

पूर्व स्वास्थ्य मंत्री तेज प्रताप यादव ने चुनाव आयोग और बिहार सरकार से औरंगाबाद स्थित अपनी करोड़ों की संपत्ति की सही जानकारी जान-बूझकर छुपा ली। इस के खिलाफ भाजपा की ओर से चुनाव आयोग से शिकायत कर लोक प्रतिनिधित्व एक्ट और कानून की विभिन्न धाराओं में कारगर कार्रवाई कर तेज प्रताप यादव की विधानसभा की सदस्यता समाप्त करने की माँग की गई है।

मालूम हो कि स्वास्थ्य, पर्यावरण एवं वन तथा लघु जल संसाधन विभाग के मंत्री रहे तेज प्रताप यादव ने औरंगाबाद में 16 जनवरी, 2010 को सात लोगों, यथा—सीता देवी, बिनेश्वर शाह, फूलमती देवी, सरस्वती देवी, जिलाल यादव एवं अनीता कुमारी (इनके नाम से दो डीड हैं) से 53 लाख 34 हजार रुपए में 45.24 डिसमिल जमीन खरीदी थी। इस जमीन की रजिस्ट्री तेज प्रताप यादव ने अपने नाम से कराई थी।

तेज प्रताप यादव की यह जमीन मौजा-शाहपुर टोले कामा बिगहा, थाना नं. 566, तौजी-4967, थाना नगर औरंगाबाद अंचल एवं जिला औरंगाबाद नगर

परिषद् क्षेत्र औरंगाबाद वर्तमान वार्ड न. 26 में अवस्थित है।

2 फरवरी, 2012 को इस जमीन को गिरवी रखकर मध्य बिहार ग्रामीण बैंक, औरंगाबाद से 2 करोड़ 29 लाख 60 हजार रुपए का कर्ज लिया गया। वर्तमान में इस जमीन पर लारा डिस्ट्रीब्यूटर्स प्रा.लि. का भवन बना हुआ है और इसमें हीरो होंडा मोटरसाइकिल का शोरूम है।

तेज प्रताप यादव ने वर्ष 2015 के बिहार विधानसभा चुनाव के उम्मीदवार के तौर पर दिए गए संपत्ति के ब्योरे में औरंगाबाद की इस जमीन और इस पर प्राप्त ऋण संबंधी तथ्य को छुपा लिया। साथ ही, वर्ष 2016 में बिहार सरकार को अपनी संपत्ति के संबंध में दिए गए ब्योरे में भी उन्होंने इसका उल्लेख नहीं किया।

दरअसल, औरंगाबाद में हाई-वे पर अवस्थित इतनी महत्त्वपूर्ण जमीन संबंधी तथ्य का उल्लेख चुनाव आयोग तथा राज्य सरकार को दिए गए संपत्ति के ब्योरे में नहीं करना धोखाधड़ी एवं जान-बूझकर बेनामी संपत्ति को छुपाने का आपराधिक प्रयास था।

चुनाव आयोग से तेज प्रताप की सदस्यता रद्द करने की माँग

सुशील कुमार मोदी के नेतृत्व में 3 जुलाई, 2017 को भाजपा के एक प्रतिनिधि मंडल ने मुख्य चुनाव आयुक्त नसीम जैदी को ज्ञापन दिया, जिसमें तेज प्रताप यादव द्वारा झूठा शपथ-पत्र देने के आरोप में आर.पी. एक्ट की धारा 125ए, आई.पी.एस. की 177 एवं Cr.P.C. की धारा 195 के तहत आपराधिक मुकदमा दर्ज करने और संविधान की धारा 324 के तहत प्रदत्त असीमित शक्तियों का उपयोग करते हुए उनकी सदस्यता रद्द करने की माँग की गई। प्रतिनिधिमंडल में प्रदेश उपाध्यक्ष व सांसद डॉ. संजय जायसवाल, सांसद सतीश चंद्र दुबे और अधिवक्ता राजेश वर्मा शामिल थे।

*औरंगाबाद में तेज प्रताप यादव की जमीन पर बनी
बिल्डिंग जिसमें है हीरो मोटरसाइकिल का शो रूम*

तेज प्रताप ने इस जमीन की रजिस्ट्री वर्ष 2010 में सात अलग-अलग दस्तावेजों के जरिए कराई तथा इसके लिए आई.सी.आई.सी.आई. बैंक, नई दिल्ली के चेक से भुगतान किया।

इस जमीन पर 2 करोड़ 29 लाख रुपए का कर्ज भी लिया है, मगर जान-बूझकर वर्ष 2015 में चुनाव आयोग को दाखिल शपथ-पत्र में इन सभी तथ्यों को छुपा लिया।

शपथ-पत्र में तेज प्रताप यादव ने लिखा है कि "मैं......... घोषणा करता हूँ कि इस शपथ-पत्र की विषय-वस्तु मेरी सर्वोत्तम जानकारी और विश्वास के अनुसार सत्य एवं सही है और इसका कोई भाग मिथ्या नहीं है तथा इसमें कोई भी तथ्य नहीं छुपाया गया है।"

□

औरंगाबाद में तेज प्रताप यादव द्वारा खरीदी गई जमीन का ब्योरा

1	Aurangabad view details	Serial No. 483 Deed No. 471 Token No. 484 Reg year-2010	Sita Devi Tej Pratap Yadav	Executant Claimant	Bharat Saw Lalu Prasad	Circle Aurangabad Municipal Mauza: Ward No. 6 Khata: 427/297 Plot: 2096/1267 Area (in Decimal): 2.4166 Land Type: Comm. Resi Mix Branch Road Land Value: 3,91,489 MVR Value: 1,62,000
2	Aurangabad view details	Serial No. 482 Deed No. 470 Token No. 486 Reg year-2010	Bineshwar Saw Tej Pratap Yadav	Executant Claimant	Ganauri Saw Lalu Prasad	Circle Aurangabad Municipal Mauza: Ward No. 6 Khata: 427/297 Plot: 2096/1267 Area (in Decimal): 2.4166 Land Type: Comm. Resi Mix Branch Road Land Value: 3,91,489 MVR Value: 1,62,000
3	Aurangabad view details	Serial No. 481 Deed No. 469 Token No. 485 Reg year-2010	Fulmati Devi Tej Pratap Yadav	Executant Claimant	Nageswar Saw Lalu Prasad	Circle Aurangabad Municipal Mauza: Ward No. 6 Khata: 427/297 Plot: 2096/1267 Area (in Decimal): 2.4166 Land Type: Comm. Resi Mix Branch Road Land Value: 3,91,489 MVR Value: 1,62,000
4	Aurangabad view details	Serial No. 480 Deed No. 468 Token No. 489 Reg year-2010	Saraswati Devi Tej Pratap Yadav	Executant Claimant	Shiv Kumar Sharma Lalu Prasad	Circle Aurangabad Municipal Mauza: Ward No. 6 Khata: 75 Plot: 1262 Area (in Decimal): 5 Land Type: Comm. Public Road Land Value: 5,25,000 MVR Value: 1,05,000

5	Aurangabad view details	Serial No. 479 Deed No. 467 Token No. 490 Reg year-2010	Jilal Yadav Tej Pratap Yadav	Executant Claimant	Basu Yadav Lalu Prasad	Circle Aurangabad Municipal Mauza: Ward No. 6 Khata: 75 Plot: 1262 Area (in Decimal): 1.50 Land Type: Comm. Public Road Land Value: 1,57,500 MVR Value: 1,05,000
6	Aurangabad view details	Serial No. 478 Deed No. 466 Token No. 488 Reg year-2010	Anita Kumari Tej Pratap Yadav	Executant Claimant	Ram Pravesh Tiwari Lalu Prasad	Circle Aurangabad Municipal Mauza: Ward No. 6 Khata: 297 Plot: 1267 Area (in Decimal): 6.50 Land Type: Comm. Resi Mix Branch Road Land Value: 10,53,000 MVR Value: 1,62,000
7	Aurangabad view details	Serial No. 477 Deed No. 465 Token No. 487 Reg year-2010	Anita Kumari Tej Pratap Yadav	Executant Claimant	Ram Pravesh Tiwari Lalu Prasad	Circle Aurangabad Municipal Mauza: Ward No. 6 Khata: 75 Plot: 1262 Area (in Decimal): 25 Land Type: Comm. Resi Mix Branch Road Land Value: 3,91,489 MVR Value: 1,62,000

झूठे शपथ-पत्र के खिलाफ मुकदमा

राजद विधायक व पूर्व मंत्री तेज प्रताप यादव द्वारा औरंगाबाद में 53 लाख 34 हजार रुपयों में खरीदी गई 45.24 डिसमिल जमीन का विवरण वर्ष 2015 में चुनाव आयोग को दिए गए शपथ-पत्र में छुपाने और जनता को धोखा देने के आरोप में भाजपा के विधान पार्षद सूरज नंदन प्रसाद ने पटना के मुख्य न्यायिक दंडाधिकारी की अदालत में 13 सितंबर, 2017 को मुकदमा संख्या 3838(सी)/2017 दर्ज कराकर लोक प्रतिनिधित्व अधिनियम की धारा 125 ए और आई.पी.सी. की धारा 193 के अंतर्गत संज्ञान लेने तथा राजद विधायक के खिलाफ गैर-जमानती वारंट जारी कर कोर्ट में उपस्थित कराने और सुनवाई प्रारंभ कर उन्हें कड़ी-से-कड़ी सजा देने का निवेदन किया है।

भाजपा विधान पार्षद ने अपनी शिकायत में कहा है कि महुआ (वैशाली) के राजद विधायक तेज प्रताप यादव ने औरंगाबाद में 16 जनवरी, 2010 को सात लोगों से अलग-अलग डीड के जरिए आई.सी.आई.सी.आई. बैंक की कनॉट प्लेस, नई दिल्ली ब्रांच के चेक से 53 लाख 34 हजार रुपए का भुगतान कर 45.24 डिसमिल जमीन खरीदी, मगर वर्ष 2015 में चुनाव आयोग को दिए गए संपत्ति के ब्योरे में जान-बूझकर इस संपत्ति को छुपा लिया जबकि इस जमीन पर फिलहाल लारा डिस्ट्रीब्यूटर्स प्रा.लि. की ओर से हीरो होंडा का शोरूम चल रहा है। दरअसल जानबूझकर संपत्ति के ब्योरे को छुपाना न केवल चुनाव आयोग को धोखा देना है, बल्कि लोक प्रतिनिधित्व की धारा 125ए का भी उल्लंघन है।

लोक प्रतिनिधित्व अधिनियम की धारा 125ए के अंतर्गत जहाँ जानबूझकर तथ्य छुपाने व झूठे शपथ-पत्र दाखिल करने पर सदस्यता समाप्त करने, वहीं आई.पी.सी. की धारा 193 के अंतर्गत सात साल तक की सजा का प्रावधान है। इस मामले में भाजपा विधायक अरुण कुमार सिन्हा और सुमन कुमार झा गवाह हैं।

In the Court of Chief Judicial Magistrate, Patna
Complaint Case No. 3838(C) of 2017

Name of the Complainant	Suraj Nandan Prasad son of Shri Ram Deo Prasad [aged about 60 years], Resident of Flat No. 204, Meena Complex, Rampur Road, P.S. Bahadurpur, Town and District Patna-800006
Name of Accused Persons	Tej Pratap Yadav son of Shri Lalu Prasad Yadav, Resident of 10, Circular Road, P.S. Sachivalaya, District Patna
Date of Occurrene	04.10.2015, till date
Place of Occurrence	Collectorate, Patna
Offences u/s	Under Section 125A of the Representation of Peoples Act, 1951 Read with Section 193 of the Indian Penal Code.
Name of the Witnesses	1] Arun Kumar Sinha S/o Late Mahendra Kumar Sinha, Flat No. 101, Ram Bilas Enclave, New Area Kadam Kuan, Lohanipur, P.S. Kadam kuan, Dist. Patna.
	2] Suman Kumar Jha S/o Ram Krishna Jha, R/o Jafarpur, P.O. Babhgi, Bhaiya Durga Gunj, P.S. Dagarua, District Purnea.

□

बड़े भाई होने के बावजूद मात्र 26 भूखंडों एवं 2 मकान परंतु 20 लाख की मोटरसाइकिल एवं 30 लाख की BMW के मालिक तेज प्रताप

- औरंगाबाद (बिहार) 7 प्लॉट (54 डिसमिल) के मालिक जिसपर Lara Interiors का Hero Honda का शोरूम चल रहा है।
- पटना के 136 डिसमिल जमीन जिस पर Lara Automobiles का पेट्रोल पंप चल रहा था, जिसे न्यायालय के आदेश से बंद कर दिया गया है।
- स्व. रघुनाथ झा एवं श्रीमती कांति सिंह द्वारा गोपालगंज एवं पटना में दान में मिला दो मंजिला मकान में तेजस्वी के साथ बराबर की हिस्सेदारी।
- पटना, गोपालगंज, औरंगाबाद में कृषि, आवासीय, व्यवसायिक 22 भूखंड के मालिक।
- 20 लाख की अमेरीकी मोटर साइकिल Harley Davidson एवं 30 लाख की BMW कार के मालिक।
- पूर्व विधान पार्षद मो. शमीम एवं राकेश रंजन तथा उनकी पत्नियों द्वारा वसीयत किए हुए पटना के 4 प्लॉट।
- तेज प्रताप यादव Shivoaham Entertainment Pvt. Ltd., में कुमार प्रिय रंजन तथा छोटू छलिया के साथ Director एवं शेयरधारक है। 5 जुलाई, 2016 को निबंधित कंपनी की रजिस्टर्ड आफिस "लालूजी का गौशाला, आर.पी.एस. के पास कृष्ण गोकुल रोड, दानापुर, पटना" दिखलाया गया है।

- पटना के दो मंजिला टिस्को गेस्ट हाउस को जिस Fairgrow Holding नामक कंपनी के माध्यम से खरीदा गया, उसके एक डायरेक्टर तेज प्रताप भी हैं।
- AK Infosystems जिसके 11 प्लाट प्रवर्तन निदेशालय ने जब्त कर लिया है, के डायरेक्टर अमित कत्याल ने तेज प्रताप को 55.51 लाख कर्ज दिए, जिसे कभी लौटाया नहीं गया, बल्कि कंपनी द्वारा Write off कर दिया गया।

□

राजद के पूर्व मंत्री के मॉल में लालू की दूसरी बेटी रोहिणी आचार्य की संपत्ति

राजद के साहिबपुर कमाल से 5 बार विधायक एवं लालू शासनकाल में लंबे समय तक नगर विकास मंत्री रहे श्री नारायण यादव के मॉल 'प्रेमश्री भरतिया जी.वी. मॉल' बोरिंग रोड, पटना की चौथी मंजिल पर अत्यंत सस्ते दाम पर लालू की दूसरी बेटी डॉ. रोहिणी आचार्य को 983 वर्गफुट का ऑफिस लिख दिया गया।

पटना के अत्यंत महत्त्वपूर्ण बोरिंग रोड मुख्य सड़क पर अवस्थित मॉल का नामकरण श्री नारायण यादव के 'श्री' और उनकी पत्नी प्रेमा देवी के 'प्रेमा' को मिलाकर 'प्रेमश्री भरतिया मॉल' किया गया है।

इस मॉल के निर्माणकर्ता M/S PREMA SHREE INFRA एक पार्टनर-शिप फर्म है, जिसमें श्री नारायण यादव की पत्नी प्रेमा देवी के नाम से 15 लाख 93 हजार के शेयर हैं। M/S PREMA SHREE INFRA का रजिस्टर्ड पता A/38 इंद्रपुरी कालोनी, राजा बाजार पटना है, जो श्री नारायण यादव का 1992 में निर्मित मकान का पता है।

श्री नारायण यादव की पहचान छिपाने के लिए निबंधित दस्तावेज में श्री नारायण यादव के स्थान पर श्री नारायण आजाद लिखा गया है।

श्री नारायण यादव यदि सीधे संपत्ति रोहिणी को बेचते तो कई तरह के सवाल पैदा हो सकते थे। अत: पहले संपत्ति किसी सुजीत सिंघानिया को 24 मार्च, 2013 को बेचा दिखाया गया और मात्र 10 माह बाद उसी संपत्ति को रोहिणी आचार्य को बेचा हुआ दिखाया गया।

श्री सुजीत सिंघानिया को 72 लाख 71 हजार बाजार मूल्य की संपत्ति को मात्र 23 लाख 10 हजार में बेचा दिखलाया गया।

श्री सुजीत सिंघानिया ने उस ऑफिस स्पेस को मात्र 10 माह बाद 58

पटना के बोरिंग रोड स्थित प्रेमश्री भरतिया जी.वी. मॉल में लालू की बेटी रोहिणी आचार्य का ऑफिस स्पेस

लाख 98 हजार में बेच दिया, जबकि उस समय उसका सरकारी बाजार मूल्य 98 लाख 99 हजार था।

प्रश्न है कि—

- आखिर सुजीत सिंघानिया से खरीद के मात्र 10 माह के भीतर रोहिणी आचार्य ने दोगुने दाम पर ऑफिस क्यों खरीद लिया?
- श्री नारायण यादव ने दस्तावेजों में अपना नाम क्यों छिपाया?

- किस एहसान के बदले लालू प्रसाद की चौथी पुत्री रोहिणी आचार्य को उपकृत किया गया?
- 98 लाख बाजार मूल्य की संपत्ति को मात्र आधे दाम पर क्यों बेच दिया गया?
- रोहिणी आचार्य को सीधे बेचने के बजाए पहले सुजीत सिंघानिया और फिर सुजीत के माध्यम से रोहिणी को बेचने के पीछे की मंशा क्या थी?
- आयकर अधिनियम के अंतर्गत सरकारी बाजार मूल्य पर ही आय कर अदा किया जाता है। क्या सुजीत और रोहिणी आचार्य ने सरकारी बाजार मूल्य पर कर अदा किया है?

□

671 डिसमिल की मालकिन लालू की चौथी बेटी रागिनी

- फरवरी 2010 में यानी शादी के 2 वर्ष पूर्व लालू प्रसाद की चौथी बेटी डॉ. रागिनी पटना शहर की 6 एकड़ 71 डिसमिल जमीन की मालकिन बन गई।
- सुश्री रागिनी पुत्री श्री लालू प्रसाद ने एक ही दिन यानी, 22 फरवरी, 2010 को श्रीमती चंद्रिका देवी पत्नी श्री विनय कृष्ण सिंह एवं श्री प्रमोद कुमार सिन्हा जे.-123 पीपुल्स कोऑपरेटिव कॉलोनी, कंकड़बाग, पटना से कुल 401 डिसमिल जमीन 31 लाख 39 हजार रुपए में खरीद लिया।
- उसी प्रकार मात्र 4 दिन बाद, यानी 26 फरवरी, 2010 को चंद्रिका देवी एवं प्रमोद कुमार सिन्हा जे.-123 पीपुल्स कोऑपरेटिव कॉलोनी, पटना से पुनः 270 डिसमिल जमीन 21 लाख 10 हजार रुपए में खरीद लिया।
- यानी 22 और 26 फरवरी, 2010 के बीच रागिनी ने कुल 671 डिसमिल जमीन 52 लाख 49 हजार में खरीद लिया।
- यह सारी जमीन पटना शहर से सटे मौजा—अब्दुल्लाहपुर महमदा, थाना-गौरीचक, जिला-पटना के अंतर्गत हैं।

□

श्रीमती चंद्रिका देवी पत्नी श्री विनय कृष्ण सिंह से रागिनी ने खरीदा

तौजी नं.	खाता नं.	सर्वे प्लाट नं.	एराजी
6422	169	509	35 डिस.
6422	176	513	38 डिस.
6422	184	514	15 डिस.
6422	182	515	20 डिस.
6422	188	465	9 डिस.
15924	86	175	55 डिस.
15924	86	176	54 डिस.
15924	86	177	26 डिस.
15924	153	218	29 डिस.
15924	129	220	30 डिस.
15924	103	221	12 डिस.

प्रमोद कुमार सिन्हा वल्द-स्व. विनय कृष्ण सिंह से रागिनी ने खरीदा

तौजी नं.	खाता नं.	सर्वे प्लाट नं.	एराजी
6422	176	507	52 डिस.
6422	188	508	19 डिस.
6422	200	520	17 डिस.
6422	204	538	65 डिस.
6422	208	539	27 डिस.
6422	169	540	26 डिस.

6422	169	541	17 डिस.
6422	226	542	26.5 डिस.
6422	195	543	38 डिस.
6307	152	179	33 डिस.

- आखिर रागिनी के पास 52 लाख 49 हजार रुपए कहाँ से आए, जिसके बदौलत वह 671 डिसमिल जमीन की मालिक बनी; जिसकी कीमत आज करोड़ों में है।

□

राबड़ी-लालू और उनके परिजनों के फ्लैट व प्लॉट

श्रीमती राबड़ी देवी पटना में 18 फ्लैट्स की मालकिन

नौकरी के एवज में ली गई थी जमीन

बिहार की पूर्व मुख्यमंत्री श्रीमती राबड़ी देवी पटना शहर के अंदर 18 फ्लैट्स एवं 18 पार्किंग स्थलों की मालकिन हैं। ये 18 फ्लैट्स कुल 18,652 वर्ग फीट में बने हैं, जिनकी वे मालकिन हैं और जिसकी कीमत आज 20 करोड़ रुपए से ज्यादा है।

श्रीमती राबड़ी देवी ने पटना शहर के दो अलग-अलग स्थानों पर लालू प्रसाद के रेलमंत्री या स्वयं के मुख्यमंत्रित्व काल में संपत्ति हासिल की।

माँ मरछिया देवी कॉम्प्लेक्स

- जलालपुर, रंजन पथ, पटना की 20.074 डिसमिल जमीन पर 21 फरवरी, 2011 को अमरेंद्र कुमार सिन्हा, खजांची रोड, पटना की कंपनी श्रेया कंस्ट्रक्शन के साथ डेवलपमेंट एग्रीमेंट किया गया। इस जमीन पर कुल 20 फ्लैट्स बनाए गए, जिसमें दूसरे फ्लोर पर 201, 202, 203, 204, 205 तथा चौथे फ्लोर पर 401, 402, 403, 404 कुल 10 फ्लैट्स की मालकिन राबड़ी देवी बन गईं।
- श्रीमती राबड़ी देवी ने जलालपुर, रंजन पथ की जमीन तीन ऐसे लोगों से लिखवाई, जिनके परिवार को रेलवे में नौकरी दी गई थी। इसमें से एक जमीन स्व. अरविंद कुमार यादव के बेटों—मनोज, गोपी कृष्ण, राजेश कुमार, विनोद कुमार एवं सुशीला देवी (पति—अरविंद यादव) से लिखवाई गई। इसमें श्री मनोज कुमार के परिवार को रेलवे में नौकरी दी गई है।
- अरविंद यादव के परिवार को आवामी को-ऑपरेटिव बैंक के माध्यम से 12 लाख 25 हजार रुपए के चेक से भुगतान दिखाया गया।
- आवामी को-ऑपरेटिव बैंक के अध्यक्ष श्री अनवर अहमद हैं, जिन्हें लालू प्रसाद का 'कबाब मंत्री' कहा जाता था। उन्हें लालू प्रसाद ने एम.एल.सी. बनवाया। उनके यहाँ सी.बी.आई. ने पिछले दिनों नोटबंदी के दौरान फर्जी बैंक खातों के आरोप में छापेमारी कर करोड़ों रुपए जब्त किए थे।
- इस प्रकार, रेलवे में नौकरी के एवज में अरविंद यादव के बेटों से लिखवाई गई जमीन पर 10,782 वर्ग फीट में बने 10 फ्लैट्स और 10 पार्किंग स्थलों की मालकिन राबड़ी देवी बन गईं।

जलालपुर, रंजन पथ, पटना स्थित राबड़ी देवी की माँ मरछिया देवी कॉम्प्लेक्स

शेखपुरा, पटना के इस अपार्टमेंट में हैं राबड़ी देवी के 8 फ्लैट्स

शेखपुरा, पटना में 8 फ्लैट्स की मालकिन राबड़ी देवी

राबड़ी देवी के मुख्यमंत्रित्व काल तथा लालू प्रसाद के रेलमंत्रित्व काल में खरीद जमीन की दिखलाई गई है। शेखपुरा, थाना शास्त्रीनगर, वार्ड नं. 3, पटना में 15.42 डिसमिल जमीन पर श्रेया कंस्ट्रक्शन के साथ मिलकर 7,920 वर्गफीट बिल्डअप एरिया के 8 फ्लैट्स तथा 8 पार्किंग स्थल की मालकिन राबड़ी देवी हैं।

इन दोनों भूखंडों पर फरवरी 2011 में श्रेया कंस्ट्रक्शन द्वारा श्री अमरेंद्र कुमार सिन्हा (खजांची रोड, पटना) के साथ डेवलपमेंट एग्रीमेंट किया गया। इस एग्रीमेंट के अनुसार, कुल 37 हजार 405 वर्गफीट में 36 फ्लैट्स बनाए जाने थे, जिसमें दोनों की 50-50 प्रतिशत हिस्सेदारी थी। इस प्रकार श्रीमती राबड़ी देवी 18 फ्लैट्स एवं 18 पार्किंग स्थलों की मालकिन बन गईं।

☐

लालू-बालू का रिश्ता

बालू माफिया ने खरीदे राबड़ी देवी के 8 फ्लैट्स

लालू प्रसाद यादव का दाहिना हाथ माने जानेवाले बालू माफिया सुभाष प्रसाद यादव ने बालू का कारोबार करनेवाली अपनी दो कंपनियों तथा अपनी पत्नी लालति देवी के नाम से चलनेवाली एक अन्य कंपनी के नाम से लालू प्रसाद यादव की माँ के नाम पर बने मरछिया देवी कमर्शियल कॉम्पलेक्स के तीन फ्लैट्स 1 करोड़ 72 लाख रुपए का भुगतान कर एक ही दिन (13 जून, 2017 को) खरीद लिये।

उसी दिन एक अन्य बालू माफिया तथा संदेश क्षेत्र के राजद विधायक अरुण यादव ने भी माँ मरछिया देवी कॉम्पलेक्स में 2 करोड़ 56 लाख 76 हजार रुपयों का भुगतान कर राबड़ी देवी के पाँच फ्लैट्स खरीद लिये।

राबड़ी देवी के फ्लैट्स की खरीद बालू माफिया द्वारा तब की गई, जब लालू परिवार की बेनामी संपत्तियों का लगातार खुलासा हो रहा था। दरअसल, आयकर के अटैचमेंट के डर से लालू प्रसाद की ओर से राबड़ी देवी की बेनामी संपत्ति की खरीद बालू माफिया द्वारा दिखाई गई है।

कौन है सुभाष प्रसाद यादव ?

बालू माफिया सुभाष प्रसाद यादव ग्राम हेतनपुर, पोस्ट माधोपुर, दानापुर, पटना के रहनेवाले हैं। वे ब्रोडसन कंस्ट्रक्शन प्रा.लि., वंशीधर कंस्ट्रक्शन प्रा. लि. और मोर मुकुट प्रा.लि. कंपनी के निदेशक हैं। इन तीनों कंपनियों को राज्य के सबसे महत्त्वपूर्ण जिले पटना, भोजपुर, सारण, वैशाली, जहानाबाद और अरवल में कुल 237 करोड़ का बालू खनन का पट्टा मिला हुआ था। सुभाष यादव की इन कंपनियों को लालू प्रसाद और प्रेमचंद गुप्ता का संरक्षण प्राप्त है।

ब्रोडसन कंस्ट्रक्शन व वंशीधर कंस्ट्रक्शन के निदेशक सुभाष यादव ने

13 जून, 2017 को राबड़ी देवी के माँ मरछिया देवी कमर्शियल कॉम्पलेक्स में क्रमश: 1,271 वर्गफीट और 1,400 वर्गफीट के दो फ्लैट्स क्रमश: 52 लाख 76 हजार और 58 लाख रुपए का भुगतान कर खरीदे। इसी दिन श्री यादव ने अपनी पत्नी लालति देवी की कंपनी राधा रमण कंस्ट्रक्शन एंड मार्केटिंग प्रा. लि. के नाम से 1,493 वर्गफीट का तीसरा फ्लैट 61 लाख 82 हजार में खरीदा।

कौन है अरुण यादव ?

श्री अरुण यादव राजद अध्यक्ष लालू प्रसाद के बेहद करीबी और संदेश से राजद के विधायक हैं। अरुण यादव ने बालू की अवैध कमाई से अर्जित पैसों को अपनी कंपनी किरण दुर्गा कंस्ट्रक्शन प्रा.लि., पुत्र राजेश कुमार रंजन व दीपू कुमार तथा पत्नी किरण देवी के 2 करोड़ 56 लाख रुपए के काले धन का इस्तेमाल राबड़ी देवी के पाँच फ्लैट्स खरीदने में किया।

श्री अरुण यादव ने किरण दुर्गा कंस्ट्रक्शन प्रा.लि. का इस्तेमाल कर 10 महेंद्रा ट्रैक्टर, 2 जे.सी.बी. मशीन, 2 फोकलेन खरीदे, जिसका इस्तेमाल बालू माफिया सुभाष यादव की तीन कंपनियाँ अवैध खनन के लिए करती हैं।

श्री अरुण यादव ने कंपनी के रुपयों से 24 लाख 31 हजार रुपए में पजेरो स्पोर्ट्स कार वर्ष 2015 में खरीदी, जिसके बैंक एग्रीमेंट में सुभाष यादव ने गवाह के नाते हस्ताक्षर किए हैं।

माँ मरछिया देवी कॉम्पलेक्स, रंजन पथ, मौजा जलालपुर, दानापुर में खरीदे गए फ्लैट्स का विवरण

कंपनी	निदेशक	फ्लैट्स का रकबा	भुगतान की गई राशि
ब्रोडसन कंस्ट्रक्शन	सुभाष प्रसाद यादव	1,271 वर्गफीट	52,76,000
वंशीधर कंस्ट्रक्शन	सुभाष प्रसाद यादव	1,400 वर्गफीट	58,03,000
राधा रमण कंस्ट्रक्शन	लालति देवी पति सुभाष यादव	1,493 वर्गफीट	61,82,000
किरण दुर्गा कंस्ट्रक्शन प्रा.लि.	राजेश कुमार रंजन S/o अरुण यादव एम.एल.ए.दीपू सिंह S/o अरुण यादव एम.एल.ए. किरण देवी W/o अरुण यादव एम.एल.ए.	1,493 वर्गफीट ---------- 1,400 वर्गफीट ---------- 1,271 वर्गफीट ---------- 975 वर्गफीट ---------- 1,043 वर्गफीट	61,82,000 ---------- 58,03,000 ---------- 52,76,000 ---------- 40,69,000 ---------- 43,46,000
सभी फ्लैट्स की खरीद 13 जून, 2017 को हुई।		**कुल-8 फ्लैट्स**	**4 करोड़ 28 लाख 76 हजार रुपए**

सवाल है कि—

- आखिर बालू माफियाओं ने ही क्यों राबड़ी देवी के 8 फ्लैट्स एक ही दिन (13 जून, 2017 को) खरीद लिये?
- क्या इन बालू माफियाओं ने अवैध खनन के काले पैसे का इस्तेमाल फ्लैट्स खरीदने में किया?
- किसी बालू कंपनी को 8 फ्लैट्स खरीदने की आवश्यकता क्यों पड़ गई?

□

कुल 43 भूखंड एवं 30 फ्लैट की मालकिन राबड़ी देवी

- Delite Marketing एवं AK Infosystem के कुल 21 प्लॉट में तेजस्वी के साथ हिस्सेदार, जिसे प्रवर्तन निदेशालय ने जब्त कर लिया है।
- इसके अतिरिक्त 18 अन्य भूखंडों की भी मालकिन हैं राबड़ी देवी।
- पावर ऑफ एटॉर्नी द्वारा पूर्व विधान पार्षद श्री राकेश रजन एवं मो. शमीम तथा सीमा वर्मा, सोफिया तब्बस्सुम के 4 प्लॉट की मालकिन।
- जलालपुर, रंजन पथ पटना में 'माँ मरछिया देवी काम्पलेक्स' में 10 फ्लैट तथा 10 पार्किंग की मालकिन राबड़ी देवी।
- शेखपुरा, पटना में एक अपार्टमेंट में 8 फ्लैट की मालकिन राबड़ी देवी।
- विधान परिषद् के चतुर्थ वर्गीय कर्मचारी ललन चौधरी द्वारा दान में दिया गया चाहरदीवारी सहित पक्का मकान।
- कांति सिंह से प्राप्त 62 डिसमिल सगुना, दानापुर की जमीन पर बने अम्योदय होम्स के 12 फ्लैट की मालकिन राबड़ी देवी।
- इसके अतिरिक्त राबड़ी देवी ने 2 करोड़ 51 लाख कर्ज एवं 1.5 करोड़ अग्रिम ले रखा है।

दामाद राहुल यादव से कर्ज	1 करोड़
सुबोध कुमार से कर्ज	50 लाख
तेज प्रताप यादव से कर्ज	26 लाख 25 हजार
श्रेया कन्सट्रक्षन से कर्ज	75 लाख
राम बाबू सिंह से अग्रिम	48 लाख
बबीता कुमारी से अग्रिम	51 लाख
अनन्जय कन्सट्रक्शन से अग्रिम	50 लाख

- श्रीमती राबड़ी देवी 1 लाख रुपए मूल्य के N P Bore Rifle No. AB860271 of .315 Bore की भी मालकिन है।

□

लालू की बेटियाँ भी होड़ में शामिल

- डॉ. रोहिणी आचार्य लालू की दूसरी बेटी राजद विधायक श्री नारायण यादव के पटना स्थित मॉल में 983 वर्ग फुट की मालकिन हैं।
- लालू की चौथी बेटी रागिनी पटना के गौरीचक में 671 डिसमिल जमीन की मालिकन हैं।
- जिस डिलाइट मार्केटिंग की साढ़े 3 एकड़ जमीन पर तेजस्वी का 750 करोड़ का मॉल बन रहा था, उस कंपनी में लालू प्रसाद ने अपनी तीसरी एवं चौथी बेटी चंदा यादव एवं रागिनी लालू को 2014-16 में कंपनी का डायरेक्टर बना दिया।
- ए.के. इंफोसिस्टम्स प्रा.लि. जिसके 11 प्लॉट को प्रवर्तन निदेशालय ने जब्त कर लिया है, उस कंपनी में भी चंदा यादव एवं रागिनी लालू डायरेक्टर हैं।
- राबड़ी के मुख्य मंत्रित्व काल में ओम प्रकाश कत्याल एवं अमित कत्याल की कम्पनी आइसबर्ग इंडस्ट्रीज प्रा.लि. ने बिहटा में शराब फैक्ट्री लगाई। आइसबर्ग में लालू की तीसरी बेटी चंदा यादव भी डायरेक्टर हैं।
- Lara Interiore Pvt. Ltd. जिसका Hero Honda का औरंगाबाद में शोरूम है, में मीसा भारती (1 हजार), चंदा यादव (2 हजार), रागिनी (1 लाख) शेयर की हिस्सेदार हैं।
- AB Exports जिसके D-1088 न्यू फ्रेंड्स कॉलोनी, नई दिल्ली के 4 मंजिला मकान को प्रवर्तन निदेशालय द्वारा जब्त कर लिया गया है, में रागिनी लालू और चंदा यादव डायरेक्टर हैं।
- फेयरग्रो होल्डिंग जिसके माध्यम से पटना में टिस्को के 2 मंजिले गेस्ट हाउस पर अधिकार कर लिया गया, में भी चंदा यादव एवं रागिनी लालू डायरेक्टर है।

- इसके अतिरिक्त चंदा यादव 2012 में स्थापित Sunrise IT Infrasoft Pvt. Ltd. में भी डायरेक्टर हैं।
- लालू प्रसाद की 7वीं बेटी राज लक्ष्मी के नाम से धनौत, दानापुर, पटना में 8 कट्ठा 15 धुर जमीन की खरीद दिखलाई गई है।
- लालू प्रसाद की छठी बेटी अनुष्का या धन्नू के नाम से ग्राम-धनौत दानापुर में 6904 वर्ग फुट भूखंड खरीद गया है।
- विधान परिषद् के चतुर्थ वर्गीय कर्मचारी श्री ललन चौधरी ने पटना शहर में 62 लाख की 7.75 डिसमिल जमीन लालू प्रसाद की पाँचवीं बेटी हेमा यादव को दान कर दिया। प्रवर्तन निदेशालय इस जमीन को जब्त कर चुका है।
- रेलवे के खलासी हृदयानंद चौधरी ने भी पटना शहर की 70 लाख रुपए की 7.76 डिसमिल जमीन हेमा यादव को दान कर दिया। यह भूखंड भी प्रवर्तन निदेशालय द्वारा जब्त किया जा चुका है।

□

संपत्ति बटोरने में मीसा भारती भी पीछे नहीं

दिल्ली में 2 फार्म हाउस सहित 21 से ज्यादा संपत्ति की मालकिन

- नई दिल्ली के बिजवासन में 250 डिसमिल जमीन का फार्म हाउस, जिसे 'मिशैल पैकर्स एंड प्रिंटर्स प्रा.लि.' के माध्यम से कब्जा किया गया है। इसे प्रवर्तन निदेशालय ने जब्त कर लिया है।
- नई दिल्ली के Western Avenue H-27/1 सैनिक फार्म की 2 बीघा 8 बिस्वा जमीन मकान सहित जिसे KHK Holding Ptv. Ltd. के माध्यम से कब्जा किया गया है। इसे प्रवर्तन निदेशालय ने जब्त कर लिया है।
- श्री सुभाष चौधरी से पटना के मैनपुरा में 4 कट्ठा 11 घुर जमीन दान में प्राप्त कर लिया।
- श्रीमती चंद्रकांता देवी से भी पटना के बिहटा में 318 डिसमिल जमीन दान में हासिल कर लिया।
- इसके अतिरिक्त पटना एवं मुजफ्फरपुर में पति शैलेश सहित कुल 21 भूखंड की मालकिन हैं मीसा भारती।
- श्री शैलेश कुमार पति मीसा भारती ने Director, Society for Excellence in Education & Dev. Pvt. Ltd., 102 First Floor, Silver Arch Apart. 22, Feroz Shah Road, New Delhi की हैसियत से 31 मार्च, 2017 को मुजफ्फरपुर के कुढ़हनी, थाना-छाजन हरिशंकर में 204 डिसमिल जमीन 30 लाख में रजिस्ट्री कराई है।
- श्रीमती मीसा भारती Aegis Distributors Pvt Ltd

खगौल, पटना में Directors हैं। इस कंपनी का 2015-16 का Turnover 29 करोड़ 53 लाख दिखाया गया है। इस कंपनी ने Mishail Packers से 4 लाख तथा सुमेधा से 1 करोड़ 70 लाख का लोन ले रखा है।

- Aegis Distributors ने 1 हजार वर्ग फुट की जमीन और मकान प्रखंड-काँटी, ग्राम-मधुबन, खाता-53 मुजफ्फरपुर और तालुका-कजरा, ग्राम- मधुबन, मुजफ्फरपुर वास्तु बिहार में 1400 वर्ग फुट का एक बंगला IDBI बैंक और केनरा बैंक मुजफ्फरपुर को गिरवी रखा है।
- AK Infosystems जिसके 11 बेनामी प्लाट को प्रवर्तन निदेशालय ने जब्त कर लिया है, के डायरेक्टर अमित कत्याल लालू की बेटी मीसा भारती एवं शैलेश कुमार के साथ M/S Kingdom Hotel & Resort Pvt. Ltd. में 2006 से 2009 तक डायरेक्टर थे।

□

एम.एल.ए. को-ऑपरेटिव में पाँच प्लॉट्स का मालिक लालू परिवार

बिहार के पूर्व एवं वर्तमान सांसदों, विधायकों एवं विधान पार्षदों को पटना में आवासीय भूखंड उपलब्ध कराने के उद्देश्य से राज्य सरकार ने वर्ष 1987 में बिहार सांसद एवं विधानमंडलीय सदस्य सहकारी समिति को 15 एकड़ सरकारी जमीन उपलब्ध करवाई थी। इस समिति के माध्यम से वैसे सदस्यों को भूखंड उपलब्ध कराया जाना था, जिनका पटना में निजी आवास नहीं है, किंतु पिछले वर्षों में इस सहकारी समिति से संबंधित अनियमितता के मामले बड़े पैमाने पर सामने आए हैं।

समिति द्वारा एक से अधिक प्लॉट का आवंटन/स्थानांतरण : सहकारी समिति की उपविधि (Bye Laws) की कंडिया 45(ii) में स्पष्ट प्रावधान है कि 'किसी भी सदस्य को एक से अधिक प्लॉट लेने की अनुमति नहीं दी जाएगी।' किंतु समिति की मिलीभगत से श्री लालू प्रसाद एवं श्री जयप्रकाश नारायण यादव ने एक-एक प्लॉट पहले से आवंटित रहने के बावजूद एक-एक अतिरिक्त प्लॉट अपने नाम से लिखवा लिया।

श्री लालू प्रसाद को वर्ष 1992 में प्लॉट संख्या 208 आवंटित किया गया था। श्री बादशाह प्रसाद आजाद को दूसरी बार एम.एल.सी. बनाने के एवज में 29 जनवरी, 2010 को श्री प्रसाद ने श्री आजाद से एक और प्लॉट संख्या 207 अपने नाम लिखवा लिया।

इसी प्रकार, श्री जयप्रकाश नारायण यादव ने प्लॉट संख्या 222 आवंटित रहने के बावजूद एक और प्लॉट संख्या 223 अपने नाम ट्रांसफर करवा लिया।

सहकारी समिति को एक से अधिक प्लॉट किसी को आवंटित या स्थानांतरित करने का अधिकार नहीं है। यदि कोई सदस्य अपना प्लॉट बेचना चाहे, तब नियमानुसार उन्हें अपना प्लॉट सहकारी समिति को सरेंडर करना

होगा, ताकि प्रतीक्षारत सदस्यों को इसका लाभ दिया जा सके।

जब प्लॉट के लिए बड़ी संख्या में सदस्यगण प्रतीक्षा सूची में थे, तब श्री लालू प्रसाद एवं श्री जयप्रकाश नारायण यादव को एक-एक अतिरिक्त प्लॉट का लीज कैसे ट्रांसफर कर दिया गया?

श्रीमती राबड़ी देवी ने मुख्यमंत्री पद का लाभ उठाकर पूर्व मंत्री स्व. सुधा श्रीवास्तव से 7 नवंबर, 2002 को 2,422 वर्ग फीट का प्लॉट नं. 151 बाउंड्री वॉल एवं बोरिंग सहित लाखों की जमीन को मात्र 72 हजार रुपए में अपने नाम लिखवा लिया।

कुछ ही महीनों के बाद 1 सितंबर, 2003 को मुख्यमंत्री रहते श्रीमती राबड़ी देवी ने तत्कालीन मंत्री श्री अब्दुल बारी सिद्दीकी को प्लॉट नं. 151 देकर उनसे अत्यंत महत्त्वपूर्ण लोकेशन पर स्थित प्लॉट नं. 209 मात्र 37 हजार रुपयों में लिखवा लिया।

प्लॉट आवंटन की मनमानी प्रक्रिया : सहकारी समिति द्वारा राष्ट्रीय जनता दल के कोषाध्यक्ष और सांसद श्री प्रेमचंद गुप्ता को प्लॉट संख्या-211 के आवंटन की स्वीकृति 8 अप्रैल, 2006 को दी गई; जबकि इससे पूर्व ही डीड निबंधन कर दिया गया और उन्होंने उस पर निर्माण कार्य भी करवा लिया। इस संबंध में विचारणीय है कि—

(i) श्री प्रेमचंद गुप्ता को आवंटित प्लॉट वर्ष 2006 तक क्यों खाली रखा गया, जबकि पहले से अनेक सदस्य प्लॉट के लिए प्रतीक्षारत थे?

(ii) प्लॉट आवंटन हेतु किस प्रक्रिया का अनुसरण किया गया?

(iii) प्लॉट आवंटन हेतु निर्धारित मापदंड क्या थे?

सामुदायिक भवन के स्थान में परिवर्तन : श्रीमती राबड़ी देवी के प्लॉट के बगल का प्लॉट संख्या-210 सामुदायिक भवन के लिए चिह्नित किया गया था; किंतु उनकी सुविधा को देखते हुए उसे श्री साधु यादव को आवंटित कर दिया गया, ताकि श्रीमती राबड़ी देवी और श्री लालू प्रसाद इस प्लॉट का भी इस्तेमाल कर सकें।

लालू प्रसाद के प्लॉट संख्या-208 में बने इसी मकान में चलता है गृह मंत्रालय के सशस्त्र सीमा बल (SSB) का जोनल पे एंड अकाउंट ऑफिस

इस प्रकार, लालू प्रसाद का परिवार एक साथ एम.एल.ए. को-ऑपरेटिव के पाँच फ्लैट्स के डिफेक्टो मालिक बन गए हैं।

प्लॉट नं. 207	बादशाह प्रसाद आजाद से एम.एल.सी. बनाने के एवज में लिखवाया
प्लॉट नं. 208	लालू प्रसाद को विधायक के नाते सन् 1992 में आवंटित
प्लॉट नं. 209	राबड़ी देवी ने पहले स्व. सुधा श्रीवास्तव और फिर श्री अब्दुल बारी सिद्दीकी से लिखवा लिया
प्लॉट नं. 210	सामुदायिक भवन के लिए आवंटित प्लॉट, जिसे बाद में साधु यादव को आवंटित किया गया
प्लॉट नं. 211	श्री प्रेमचंद गुप्ता को वर्ष 2006 में आवंटित प्लॉट

लीज ट्रांसफर में काले धन का उपयोग : सहकारी समिति द्वारा वर्ष 1992 में आवंटित जिस भूखंड की कीमत 37 हजार रुपए थी, उसे श्री बादशाह प्रसाद आजाद ने बीस वर्षों के बाद भी उसी कीमत (अर्थात् 37 हजार रुपए) में श्री लालू प्रसाद को ट्रांसफर कर दिया। इसी प्रकार, श्रीमती राबड़ी देवी, श्री जयप्रकाश नारायण यादव एवं अन्य लोगों को भी 37 हजार रुपए में ही लीज का ट्रांसफर किया गया; जबकि उस प्लॉट का बाजार मूल्य लाखों रुपए में है। इस बात की पूरी आशंका है कि इस लेन-देन में व्यापक पैमाने पर काले धन का उपयोग किया गया।

आवासीय भवनों का व्यावसायिक उपयोग : बिहार सरकार ने सहकारी समिति को जमीन केवल आवासीय उपयोग हेतु भूखंड आवंटित करने के लिए दी थी, किंतु श्री लालू प्रसाद सहित अनेक लोग इसका व्यावसायिक उपयोग कर रहे हैं, जो लीज की शर्तों का उल्लंघन है। श्री लालू प्रसाद जब रेलमंत्री थे, तब से ही उनके प्लॉट संख्या-208 में गृह मंत्रालय के सशस्त्र सीमा बल (SSB) का जोनल पे एंड अकाउंट ऑफिस चल रहा है और पंद्रह वर्षों से नियमों की धज्जियाँ उड़ाकर वह लाखों रुपए कमा रहे हैं। इसी प्रकार, अनेक लोगों ने अपने घरों को किराए पर लगा रखा है।

खास महाल नीति, 2011, बिहार सहकारिता समिति अधिनियम, 1935 एवं अन्य नियमों का उल्लंघन : खास महाल नीति, 2011, बिहार सहकारिता समिति अधिनियम, 1935, लीज की शर्तों एवं अन्य नियमों का व्यापक पैमाने पर उल्लंघन किया जा रहा है। तीस वर्षों की लीज की अवधि 31 दिसंबर, 2017 को समाप्त हो गई, जिसका नवीनीकरण किया जाना है।

लालू प्रसाद के कब्जे के प्लॉट की स्थिति

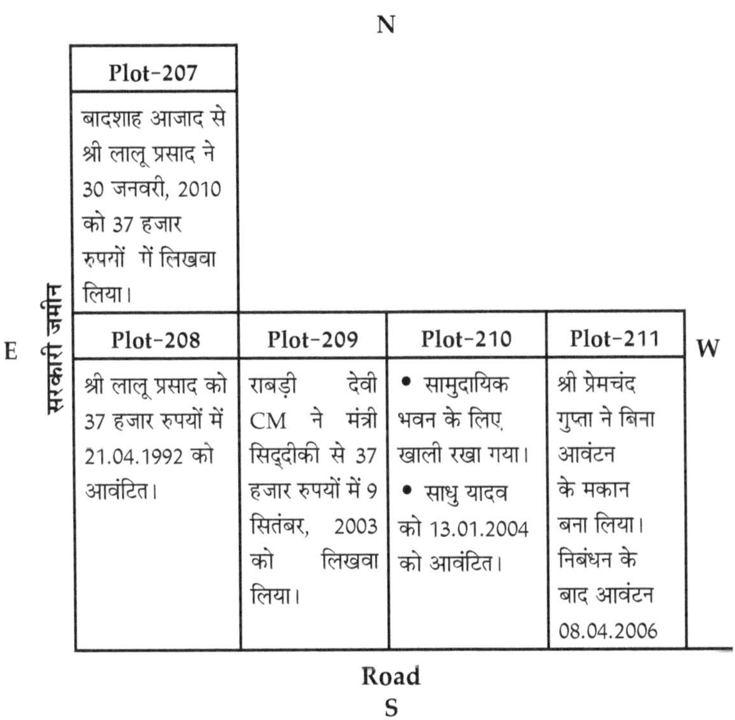

परिवार के लिए 141 भूखंड, 30 फ्लैट एवं 5 मकान अर्जित करनेवाले लालू मात्र 3 संपत्ति के मालिक

- श्री लालू प्रसाद को विधायक के नाते 1992 में 'बिहार सांसद एवं विधानमंडलीय सदस्य समिति' द्वारा समनपुरा, पटना में प्लॉट नं.-208 आवंटित किया गया, जिसपर 3 मंजिला मकान निर्मित है। प्रावधान के विपरीत वहाँ भारत सरकार के SSB का जोनल पे एंड एकाउंट आफिस किराए पर चल रहा है।
- बादशाह आजाद को विधान पार्षद बनाने के एवज में 2010 में प्लॉट नं. -207 लिखवा लिया गया, जबकि एक व्यक्ति केवल एक प्लॉट का ही हकदार था।

  इस प्लॉट की खरीद को छिपाए रखा गया। 2018 में पहली बार राबड़ी देवी के चुनावी शपथ-पत्र में इस संपत्ति का उल्लेख किया गया है।
- पटना के ग्राम-धनौत, दानापुर, पटना में 2.5 कट्ठा भूखंड के मालिक हैं लालू प्रसाद
- इसके अतिरिक्त निम्न संपत्ति के भी मालिक हैं लालू प्रसाद

Mercedes Benz Car UP-32GC-0009	40 लाख
German Make Pistol No. 11679	03 लाख
N.P. Bore Rifle No. AB860271 of .315 BORE	01 लाख

- इसके अतिरिक्त बालू माफिया सुभाष यादव से 25 लाख एवं डिलाइट मार्केटिंग के पूर्व मालिक प्रेम चंद गुप्ता से भी 15 लाख का कर्ज ले रखा है।

□

आवामी को-ऑपरेटिव बैंक लालू की दुधारू गाय

राजद के पूर्व मंत्री अनवर अहमद के आवामी को-ऑपरेटिव बैंक का इस्तेमाल लालू परिवार के काले धन को सफेद करने, ऋण प्राप्त करने, नोटबंदी के बाद लालू प्रसाद सहित राजद नेताओं के 500 और 1,000 के नोटों को बदलने जैसे काम में किया गया। आवामी को-ऑपरेटिव बैंक के चेयरमैन अनवर अहमद का प्रवेश लालू प्रसाद के रसोई घर तक था। वे लंबे समय तक उनके घर का खाना बनाते थे, जिस कारण उन्हें 'कबाब मंत्री' भी कहा जाता था। नोटबंदी के बाद आवामी को-ऑपरेटिव बैंक के 70 बेनामी खातों और अनवर अहमद के चार ट्रस्ट के खातों के माध्यम से 10-12 करोड़ रुपए के काले धन को सफेद करने के साक्ष्य मिले हैं। सी.बी.आई. और ई.डी. इस मामले की जाँच कर रही हैं।

- ये वही अनवर अहमद हैं, जिन्हें लालू प्रसाद ने राज्यपाल कोटे से एम.एल.सी. बनवाया, ताकि उनके को-ऑपरेटिव बैंक का इस्तेमाल काले धन को सफेद करने के लिए किया जा सके।
- लालू परिवार की बेनामी संपत्ति की खरीद में आवामी को-ऑपरेटिव बैंक का पूरा इस्तेमाल किया गया।
- जमीन खरीद के अनेक मामलों में आवामी को-ऑपरेटिव बैंक के माध्यम से संदिग्ध राशि का भुगतान दिखाया गया है।
- श्रीमती राबड़ी देवी का बचत खाता सं.-6651 तथा श्री लालू प्रसाद का बचत खाता सं.-1001 अभी भी आवामी को-ऑपरेटिव बैंक में क्रियाशील है।
- लालू प्रसाद के आवामी को-ऑपरेटिव बैंक के खाते में 58 लाख रुपए तथा राबड़ी देवी के इसी बैंक के एक खाते में 15.62 लाख रुपए जमा हैं।
- माँ मरछिया देवी कॉम्प्लेक्स में राबड़ी देवी के 10 फ्लैट्स जिस अरविंद यादव के परिवार की जमीन पर बने हैं, उसका भुगतान 12 लाख 25 हजार रुपए आवामी को-ऑपरेटिव बैंक के नाम से दिखलाया गया है।
- आज लालू परिवार का खटाल जिस सगुना, नया टोला के 34.21 डिसमिल जमीन पर अवस्थित है, जिसे पहले कांति सिंह ने 99 साल की लीज पर और फिर चार वर्ष बाद 'बेचा हुआ' दिखाया गया है, के लिए 19 लाख 80 हजार रुपयों का भुगतान आवामी को-ऑपरेटिव बैंक के नाम से ही दिखलाया गया है।
- आवामी को-ऑपरेटिव बैंक के अध्यक्ष श्री अनवर अहमद ने नोटबंदी के बाद 60 मजदूरों के नाम बैंक खाते खोलकर प्रत्येक में 2.30 लाख रुपए जमा कराए। बाद में 24 हजार रुपए प्रति सप्ताह प्रति खाते से निकाले गए, ताकि आयकर विभाग की निगाह से बचा जा सके।

- जिन मजदूरों के नाम से खाते खोलकर रुपए जमा कराए गए, उन्हें पता भी नहीं कि उनके नाम से खाते खोले जा रहे हैं।
- इन बेनामी खातों में 11 करोड़ रुपयों से ज्यादा की रकम जमा करने के तुरंत बाद निकाल ली गई थी।
- अनवर अहमद के ट्रस्ट में छापेमारी के दौरान 10 लाख रुपयों के नए 2,000 और 500 के नोट बरामद किए गए थे।
- अनवर ने अपने परिवार के चार ट्रस्टों का दुरुपयोग नोटबंदी के बाद 500 और 1,000 के पुराने नोट जमा करने के लिए किया।
- इन सभी ट्रस्टों का खाता आवामी को-ऑपरेटिव बैंक में था, जहाँ दिखलाया गया कि चंदे के रूप में यह राशि उन्हें मिली है।
- सी.बी.आई. ने 23 मार्च, 2018 को अनवर अहमद के बेटे और आवामी को-ऑपरेटिव बैंक के निदेशक अरशद अहमद एवं अरशद के स्कूल की प्राचार्य सुप्रिया चटर्जी को नोटबंदी में काले धन को सफेद करने के आरोप में गिरफ्तार कर लिया है।

□

तेजस्वी का 750 करोड़ का मॉल बनानेवाला सुरसण्ड से राजद का विधायक

अबू दोजाना Habitual offender

- तेजस्वी यादव के 'Biggest Mall of Bihar' को बनानेवाले राजद के सुरसण्ड विधायक अबू दोजाना द्वारा निर्माणाधीन डाक बंगला चौराहा के पास 'Patna one Mall' को पटना नगर निगम ने 6 अगस्त, 2014 को निगरानी वाद संख्या 200A/2013 में निम्न आदेश पारित किया है।
- श्री अबू दोजाना CMD मेरेडियन कंस्ट्रक्शन, पटना के द्वारा लगातार अलग-अलग जगहों पर भवन उपविधि का उल्लघंन करने के Habitual offender हैं।
- इस मामले में भी (Patna One Mall) जान-बूझकर भवन उपविधि का उल्लघंन करने के कारण उन पर दस लाख रुपए का दंड (Penalty) अधिरोपित किया जाता है।
- चूँकि स्वत्व स्पष्ट नहीं है, अत: कोई निर्माण नहीं हो सकता है।
- प्रतिवादी को आदेश दिया जाता है कि दिनांक 14 अगस्त, 2018 को पारित नक्शे से हटकर किए जा रहे निर्माण B+G+6 से ऊपर के तल्ले तथा अन्य अतिरिक्त निर्माण एवं ग्राउंड फ्लोर और प्रथम तल पर पार्किंग की व्यवस्था हेतु बनी दुकानें एक माह में अपसारित करें।
- उक्त भाग को अपसारित करने के उपरांत प्रश्नगत स्थल पर भिन्न-भिन्न न्यायालयों में लंबित स्वामित्व विवाद के निबटारा होने तक स्थल को यथा रखें।
- बिजली कनेक्शन यदि परिसर में है तो जी.एम., पेसू, निदेशित है कि 7 दिनों के भीतर इसका संबंध-विच्छेदन (Disconnct) कर दें

तथा भविष्य में बिना आदेश के कनेक्शन नहीं दें।

- जिला अवर निबंधक, पटना को आदेश दिया जाता है कि प्रश्नगत भूखंड पर निर्मित भवन के किसी अंश का निबंधन नहीं करें।
- निदेशक, शहरी योजना को निदेश दिया जाता है कि वे निबंधित वास्तुविद रमण कुमार निबंधन संख्या-47/09 पर स्थानीय थाना में प्राथमिकी दर्ज करें।
- थाना अध्यक्ष कोतवाली की यह जिम्मेवारी (Responsibility) होगी कि वे उक्त परिसर में कोई निर्माण न होने दें। यदि होता है तो अपने स्वयं के बयान पर प्राथमिकी दर्ज करें।
- कार्यपालक पदाधिकारी, नूतन राजधानी अंचल एवं कार्यपालक अभियंता, नूतन राजधानी प्रमंडल (उ.) संयुक्त रूप से निदेशित है कि उक्त परिसर में नगरीय सुविधा के तहत सीवर, वाटर सप्लाई, ड्रेनेज की सुविधा इन्हें मुहैया नहीं की जाय।

□

प्रवर्तन निदेशालय द्वारा जब्त संपत्ति

डिलाइट मार्केटिंग की जब्त की गई संपत्तियों का ब्योरा

Name of the Benamidar	Beneficial Owner	Date of Passing order u/s 24(4) of PBPT Act,1988	Description of Benami Property attached	
			Description of property	Area in decimals, 1=435.5 sq ft.
M/s Delight Marketing Pvt. Ltd.	(a) Shri Tejashwi Prasad Yadav	16.09.2017	(1) Tauzi No.5519, khata No.84, Cadestral Survey Plot No. 56, Mauza Jalalpur, Pargana Phulwari Sharif, P.S-Danapur, District Patna.	27.75 decimal
			(2) Tauzi No.5519, khata No.94, Cadestral Survey Plot No. 55, Mauza Jalalpur, Pargana Phulwari Sharif, P.S-Danapur, District Patna.	27.75 decimal
			(3) Tauzi No.5519, khata No.94, Cadestral Survey Plot No. 55, Area Mauza Jalalpur, Pargana Phulwari Sharif, P.S- Danapur, District Patna.	27.75 decimal
			(4) Tauzi No.5519, khata No.84, Cadestral Survey Plot No. 56, Area 16.75 decimal and Tauzi No.5519, khata No.94, Cadestral Survey Plot No. 57, Area 11 decimal at Mauza Jalalpur, Pargana Phulwari Sharif, P.S- Danapur, District Patna.	27.75 decimal

Name of the Benamidar	Beneficial Owner	Date of Passing order u/s 24(4) of PBPT Act,1988	Description of Benami Property attached	
			Description of property	Area in decimals, 1=435.5 sq ft.
	(b) Smt. Rabri Devi		(5) Tauzi No.5519, khata No.94, Cadestral Survey Plot No. 55, Area 25 decimal and Tauzi No.5519, khata No.90, Cadestral Survery Plot No. 54, Area 10 decimal at Mauza Jalalpur, Pargana Phulwari Sharif, P.S- Danapur, District Patna.	35 decimal
			(6) Tauzi No.5519, khata No.90, Cadestral Survey Plot No. 54, Mauza Jalalpur, Pargana Phulwari Sharif, P.S- Danapur, District Patna.	35.5 decimal
			(7) Tauzi No.5519, khata No.90, Cadestral Survey Plot No. 49, Area 33 decimal and Tauzi No.5519, khata No.90, Cadestral Survey Plot No. 54, Area 2 decimal at Mauza Jalalpur, Pargana Phulwari Sharif, P.S- Danapur, District Patna.	35 decimal

Name of the Benamidar	Beneficial Owner	Date of Passing order u/s 24(4) of PBPT Act,1988	Description of Benami Property attached	
			Description of property	Area in decimals, 1=435.5 sq ft.
			(8) Tauzi No.5519, khata No.90, Cadestral Survey Plot No. 49, Area 16.5 decimal and Tauzi No.5519, khata No.90, Cadestral Survey Plot No. 54, Area 23.75 decimal at Mauza Jalalpur, Pargana Phulwari Sharif, P.S- Danapur, District Patna.	40.25 decimal
			(9) Tauzi No.5519, khata No.90, Cadestral Survey Plot No. 49, Area 16.5 decimal and Tauzi No. 5519, khata No.90, Cadestral Survey Plot No. 54, Area 23.75 decimal at Mauza Jalalpur, Pargana Phulwari Sharif, P.S- Danapur, District Patna.	40.25 decimal
			(8) Tauzi No.5519, khata No.90, Cadestral Survey Plot No. 49, Area 16.5 decimal and Tauzi No.5519, khata No.90, Cadestral Survery Plot No. 54, Area 23.75 decimal at Muauza Jalalpur, Pargana Phulwari Sharif, P.S- Danapur, District Patna.	40.25 decimal

Name of the Benamidar	Beneficial Owner	Date of Passing order u/s 24(4) of PBPT Act,1988	Description of Benami Property attached	
			Description of property	Area in decimals, 1=435.5 sq ft.
			(9) Tauzi No.5519, khata No.90, Cadestral Survey Plot No. 49, Area 16.5 decimal and Tauzi No.5519, khata No.90, Cadestral Survey Plot No. 54, Area 23.75 decimal at Mauza Jalalpur, Pargana Phulwari Sharif, P.S- Danapur, District Patna.	40.25 decimal

ए.के. इन्फोसिस्टम्स की जब्त की गई संपत्ति का ब्योरा

Name of the Benamidar	Beneficial Owner	Date of Passing order u/s 24(4) of PBPT Act,1988	Description of Benami Property attached	
			Description of property	Area in decimals, 1=435.5 sq ft.
M/s A.K Infosystems Pvt. Ltd.	(a) Shri Tejashwi Prasad Yadav. (b) Smt. Rabri Devi	15.09.2017	(1) Tauzi No.5553, Thana No.20, Khata No.183, Part of Cadestral Survey Plot No.1161, at Mauza Ghanot Mahal Rupaspur, Thana Danapur, Pargana Phulwari Sharif, District Patna	21.875 decimal 9.845 decimal 14 decimal
			(2) Tauzi No.437, Thana No.17, Khata No.151, Part of Cadestral Survey Plot No.1616, at Mauza Chitkohra, Present Thana Gardani Bagh, District Patna.	9.845 decimal
			(3) Tauzi No.5120/15064, Thana No.17, Khata No.282, Part of Cadestral Survey Plot No.1614, at Mauza Chitkohra, Survey Thana Phulwari Shraif, Present Thana Gardani Bagh, District Patna.	14 decimal
			(4) Tauzi No.5207, Thana No.17, Khata No.151, Part of Cadestral Survey Plot No.1616, at Mauza Chitkohra, Thana Phulwari Sharif, Present Thana Gardani Bagh, District Patna.	9.845 decimal

Name of the Benamidar	Beneficial Owner	Date of Passing order u/s 24(4) of PBPT Act,1988	Description of Benami Property attached	
			Description of property	Area in decimals, 1=435.5 sq ft.
			(5) Tauzi No.437, Thana No.17, Khata No.151, Part of Cadestral Survey Plot No.1616, at Mauza Chitkohra, Thana Phulwari Sharif, Present Thana Gardani Bagh, District Patna.	9.845 decimal
			(6) Tauzi No.437, Thana No.17, Khata No.151, Part of Cadestral Survey Plot No.1616, at Mauza Chitkohra, Thana Phulwari Sharif, Present Thana Gardani Bagh, District Patna.	28.53125 decimal
			(7) Tauzi No.5404, Thana No.21, Khata No.404, (1500 part, 1502 part), Khata No. 406 (1509 part), Khata No.-413 (1514 Part), Ward No. 20/21, Part of Cadestral Survey, Plot No. 1500/1502/1509/1514, at Mauza Danapur Gola Road, Thana Danapur, District Patna.	13.7 decimal
			(8) Tauzi No.5404, Thana No.21, Khata No.404,(1500, 1501, 1502 part,), Khata No. 406 (1509 part), Khata No.-413 (1514 part), Ward No. 20/21, Part of Cadestral Survey, Plot No. 1500/1501, 1502, 1509, 1514, at Mauza Danapur Gola Road, Thana Danapur, District Patna.	27.63 decimal

Name of the Benamidar	Beneficial Owner	Date of Passing order u/s 24(4) of PBPT Act,1988	Description of Benami Property attached	
			Description of property	Area in decimals, 1=435.5 sq ft.
			(9) Tauzi No. 5404, Thana No. 21, Khata No. 404,(1500, 1501, 1502 part,), Khata No. 406 (1509 part), Khata No.-413 (1514 part), Ward No. 20/21, Part of Cadestral Survey Plot No. 1500/1501, 1502, 1509, 1514, at Mauza Danapur Gola Road, Thana Danapur, District Patna.	13.85 decimal
			(10) Tauzi No.2596, Thana No.21, Khata No.255 Part of Cadesral Survey Plot No.148, at Mohalla Salempur Dumra alias Samanpura, Police Station Shastri Nagar, District Patna.	6.41 decimal

ए.बी. एक्सपोर्ट्स की जब्त संपत्ति का ब्योरा

Name of the Benamidar	Beneficial Owner	Date of Passing order u/s 24(4) of PBPT Act,1988	Description of Benami property attached	
			Description of property	Area in decimals, 1=435.5 sq ft.
M/s AB Exports Pvt. Ltd.	(a) Shri Tejashwi Prasad Yadav (b) Ms. Chanda Yadav	08.09.2017	D-1088, New Friends Colony, New Delhi	10.332 decimal

मिशेल पैकर्स की जब्त संपत्ति का ब्योरा

Name of the Benamidar	Beneficial Owner	Date of Passing order u/s 24(4) of PBPT Act,1988	Description of Benami property attached	
			Description of property	Area in decimals, 1=435.5 sq ft.
M/s Mishail Packers & Printing Pvt. Ltd.	(a) Sh. Shailesh (b) Smt. Misha Bharti	14.09.2017	Farm No.-26, Palam Farms Vpo-Bijwasan, Near Palam Vihar Road New Delhi 110061	250 decimal

DETAILS OF PROPERTIES ATTACHED UNDER BENAMI ACT, 1988 IN THE CASES OF SMT. RABRI DEVI & SMT. HEMA YADAV

Sl. No.	Deed No. & Date	Type of Deed	Desription of the property/ transaction	Name and address of Owner/Seller/Doner	Name and address of Power of Attorney holder/Purchaser/ donee
1.	1515 dated 25/01/2014	Gift	Piece of land measuring 2.5 decimal situated at Mauja Saguna, Phulwari Sharif, Patna	Shir Lalan Chaudhary, S/o- Shri Sukar Chaudhary, Vill Siyadih, P.S. Barhariya, Distt. Siwan	Smt. Rabri Devi, W/o- Shri Lalu Prasad
2.	2032 dated 30/03/2009	Sale	Land at Saguna, Nayatola, Patna purchased by Shri Lalan Chaoudhary, S/o- Shri Sukat Chaudhary from Shri Ratneshwar Prasad Yadav. later he gifted it to Smt. Rabri Devi vide gift deed no. 1515 dated 25/01/2014 as per serial no. 1 above.	—	—

Sl. No.	Deed No. & Date	Type of Deed	Desription of the property/ transaction	Name and address of Owner/Seller/Doner	Name and address of Power of Attorney holder/Purchaser/ donee
3.	2325 dated 13/02/2014	Gift	Piece of land measuring 7.75 decimal situated at Mauza-Dhanaut, Danapur, Dist. Patna	Shri Hridaynand Chaudhary, S/o- Shri Shankar Chaudhary, Vill. Itawa, P.S. Uchkagaon, Distt. Gopaiganj	Smt. Hema Yadav W/o- Shri Vineet Yadav, Saket, New Delhi
4.	6006 dated 29/03/2008	Sale	Land at Mauza Dhanaut, Danapur. Dist. Patna purchased by Shri Hridayanand Chaudhary, S/o- Shri Shankar	—	—
			Chaudhary from Shri Brij Nandan Ray. Later he gifted it to Smt. Hema Yadav, W/o Shri Vineet Yadav vide deed no. 2325 dated to 13/02/2014 as per serial no. above.		

Sl. No.	Deed No. & Date	Type of Deed	Desription of the property/ transaction	Name and address of Owner/Seller/Doner	Name and address of Power of Attorney holder/Purchaser/ donee
5.	2327 dated 13/02/3.14	Gift	Piece of land measuring 7.75 decimals situated at Mauza-Dhanaut, Danapur, Dist. Patna.	Shri Lalan Chaudhary, S/o- Shri Sukar Chaudhary, Vill. Siyadih, P.S. Barhariya, Distt. Siwan	Smt. Hema Yadav, W/o- Shri Vineet Yadav, Saket, New Delhi.
6.	6004 dated 29/02/2008	Sale	Land at Mauza Dhanaut, Danapur, Dist. Patna purchased by Shri Lalan Chaudhary, S/o- Shri Sukat Chaudhary from Shri Vishun, Dev Raj. Later he gifted it to Smt. Hema Yadav. W\o Shri Vineet Yadav vide deed no. 2327 dated 13/02/2014 as per serial no. 5 above.	—	—

Property details of Smt. Rabari Devi			
Patna			
Agricultural Land			
Sl.	**Locations**	**Survey No.(s)**	**Area**
1	Vill- Dhanaut, P.S.- Danapur, Distt.- Patna	Khata No.-183, Plot No.-1161, Tauzi No.-5553, Thana No.-20	8 katha 15 Dhur
2	Vill.- Mahuabagh, P.S. - Phulwarishariff, Distt.-Patna	Khata No.-173,Plot No.-1548	7.75 Dec.
3	Vill.- Mahuabagh, P.S. - Phulwarishariff, Distt.-Patna	Khata No.-173,Plot No.-1548	7.75 Dec.
Non Agricultural Land			
1	Vill.-Dhanaut, P.S.- Danapur, Distt- Patna	Khata No.-189, Plot No.-1547	5 Katha
2	Mauza Samanpura, Rev. Thana-Phulwari Shariff, Present Thana- Shastrinagar, Distt.-Patna	Samiti Plot No.-209, Revenue Thana No.-12	2432 Sq Ft.
3	Mauza -Saguna, Naya Tola, P.S.-Danapur, Distt.-Patna	Khata No.-98, Khesra No.-257(P)	34.212 Dec.
Residential Building (Includig Apartments)			
1	Muza-Sheikhpura, Rev. Thana- Phulwarishariff Distt.- Patna	Khata No-403, Survey Plot No.-1016, Thana No.-9	"2 Katha, 5 Dhur Under Const. 2014"

2	Muza-Sheikhpura, Rev. Thana- Phulwarishariff, Present Thana -Gardanibagh, Distt- Patna	Khata No-396, Survey Plot No.-1019, Tauzi-no-5767, Thana No.-9	"1668 Sq Ft Under Const. 2014"
3	Muza-Sheikhpura Rev. Thana- Phulwarishariff Distt Present Thana -Gardanibagh, Distt- Patna	Khata No-384, Survey Plot No.-1015, Tauzi-no-5767, Thana No.-9	"1985 Sq ft. Under const. 2014"
4	At.- Jalalpur, P.S.- Danapur, Distt- Patna	Khata No-30, Plot No.-8, Tauzi-no-5516, Thana No.-22	"3 Katha 1 Dhur 2½ Dhurki Under Const. 2014"
5	At.- Jalalpur, P.S.- Danapur Distt- Patna	Khata No-30, Plot No.-8, Tauzi-no-5516, Thana No.-22	"3 Katha 7 Dhur, Under Const. 2014"
6	At. Vill.- Saguna, P.S.- Danapur Distt- Patna	Khata No-155, Khesra No.-277(P), Thana No.-23	"2.5 Dec. 1000 Sq ft. 2014"
Commercial Building (Includig Apartments)			
1	Mauza Saguna, Naya Tola P.S. Danapur, Distt. -Patna	Khata No.-98, Khesra No.-258(P)	"62 Dec. 18000 Sq ft 2014"

Others

1	At Mauza- Saguna, P.S.-Danapur, Dist-Patna	Tauzi No.-5233, Rev. Thana-23, Khata No.-26, Survey Plot -503, Sub. Plot-41/H	3354 Sq ft

2	At Mauza- Saguna, P.S.-Danapur, Dist-Patna	Tauzi No.-5233, Thana-23, Khata No.-22, Survey Plot -495, Sub. Plot-43/H	3372 Sq ft
3	At Mauza- Saguna P.S.-Danapur, Dist-Patna	Tauzi No.-5233, Thana-23, Khata No.-22, Survey Plot -495, Sub. Plot-42/H	3300 Sq ft
4	At Mauza- Saguna, P.S.-Danapur, Dist-Patna	Tauzi No.-5233, Thana-23, Khata No.-22, Survey Plot No. -495, Sub. Plot-44/H	3411 Sq ft
5	Dhanaut, Mahuabagh, Danapur, Patna	Khata No. 183, Plot No. 1161	3.12 Dec.
Gopalganj			
Agricultural Land			
Sl.	**Locations**	**Survey No.(s)**	**Area**
1	At.-Selarkala/Turkaha P.S. Uchakagaon Distt. - Gopalganj	Khata No-68.2(Selarkala) Plot No.-301,303,737,736 Thana No-873, Khata No-37,69,129 (Turkaha) Plot No-128,129,20,18,2 Thana No- 874	5 Bigha 1 Katha 7 Dhur

Others

1	Mauza- Amarkhem, Pargana-Kuari, PS-Mirganj, District-Gopalganj	Tauji-3296, Thana-856, Khata-121, Khesra-36	2 Katha
2	Vill-Selarkala, Thana-Phulwaria, Distt.-Gopalganj	Khata No. 56, Plot No. 11, 138, Thana No. 873	24.16 Dec.

Property details of Shri Lalu Prasad Yadav			
Patna			
1	At Vill.-Dhanaut, PS-Danapur, Distt.-Patna	Khata No. 13, Plot No. 1167, Thana No. 20	2.5 Katha
2	Mauza - Samanpura, Thana-Shatrinagar, Distt.-Patna	Samiti Plot No.206, Revenue Thana No. 12	"Land 2428 Mtr. Building - Ground + 2 Floor"
3	Mauza - Samanpura, Thana-Shastrinagar, Distt.-Patna	Samiti Plot No.207, Revenue Thana No. 10	2428 Mtr. Under Const.

Property details of Shri Tejashwi Yadav			
Gopalganj			
Agricultural Land			
Sl.	**Locations**	**Survey No.(S)**	**Area**
1	At Vill. Phulwaria, PS-Phulwaria, Distt.-Gopalganj	Plot No. 1288P, Khata No. 156	19 Dec.
2	At Vill. Phulwaria, PS-Phulwaria, Distt.-Gopalganj	Plot No. 802P, Khata No. 31	10 Katha 17 Dhur
Tejashwi Yadav Alias Tarun Prasad Yadav with Tej Pratap Yadav			
1	At Vill. Phulwaria, PS-Phulwaria, Distt.-Gopalganj	Plot No. 821, 955, 825, Khata No. 74, 123	16 Katha 5½
2	At Vill. Phulwaria, PS-Phulwaria, Distt.-Gopalganj	Plot No. 979, Khata No. 52, Tauzi No. 3296	2 Katha 5 Dhur
3	At+Vill Vishnupura, Pargana Kuari, PS-Phulwaria, Distt.-Gopalganj	Plot No. 69M, Thana No. 862, Khata No. 54, Tauzi No. 3296	3 Katha
4	4. At Vill Selarkela, PS-Phulwaria, Distt.-Gopalganj	Plot No. 99M, Thana No. 873, Khata No. 64, Tauzi No. 3296	5 Katha 6½ Dhur
5	Mauza-Phulwaria, Panchayat-Bhagwat Parsa, Distt. Gopalganj	Khata No. 74, Survey No. 892	4 Katha 8½ Dhur

Residential Building (Includig Apartments)			
1	Mauza Hajiapur PS- Gopalganj	Khata No. 155.157. Plot No. 7 & 8(Part),9	"Land 3 Katha 2½ Dhur Building Ground Floor Built up area 3000 Sqft."
		Patna	
Agricultural Land			
1	At Mauza-Planga, PS-Phulwari Sharif, Distt.-Patna	Khata No. 28, Plot No. 201, Tauzi No. 5757/18019	1 Bigha
2	At Mauza-Planga, PS-Phulwari Sharif, Distt.-Patna	Khata No. 28, Plot No. 201, Tauzi No. 5757/18019	1 Bigha
Tejashwi Yadav Alias Tarun Prasad Yadav with Tej Pratap Yadav			
1	At Vill Banya, PS-Phulwari Sharif, Distt.-Patna	Khata No. 581, 661, Plot No. 352 (P) 352/324	21 Katha 2 Dhur 7.75 Dhurki
Non Agricultural Land			
1	At.Vill Saguna, PS Danapur Distt.-Patna	Khata No. 23, Plot No. 257(Part), Thana No. 23, Tauzi No. 5292	3402 Sq ft.
2	At Vill Dhanaut, PS Danapur, Distt.-Patna	Khata No. 183, Plot No. 1161, Thana No. 20	8 Katha 15 Dhur
Commercial Building (Includig Apartments)			
1	Mauza Mazaffarpur Chitkohra PS-Gardanibagh, Distt.-Patna	Khata No.113. Survey Plot No. 1028. Tauzi No. 18215. Revenue Thana No. 17	"Land 3 Katha Building Ground Floor + 2 Floor Built up area 2000 Sqft"

Property details of Shri Tej Pratap Yadav

Gopalganj

Agricultural Land

Sl.	Locations	Survey No.(S)	Area
1	At Vill. Phulwaria, PS-Uchka Gaon, Distt-Gopalganj	Plot No. 1287/1267 & 825, Khata No. 156, Thana No. 970, Tauzi No. 3296	13 Katha 11 Dhur
2	At Vill. Selarkela, PS-Phulwaria, Distt-Gopalganj	Khata No. 16, Plot No. 776 & 777, Thana No. 873, Tauzi No. 3296	2 Katha
3	At Vill Phulwaria, PS-Uchka Gaon, Distt-Gopalganj	Khata No. 151, Plot No. 980M	11.53 Dec.
4	At Vill Phulwaria, PS-Phulwaria, Distt-Gopalganj	Khata No. 74, Plot No.982, Thana No. 870	8 Katha 17 Dhur
	"Tej Pratap Yadav Jointly with Tejashwi Prasad Alias Tarun Prasad Yadav"		
1	At Vill. Phulwaria, PS-Phulwaria, Distt.-Gopalganj	Plot No. 821, 955, 825, Khata No. 74, 123	16 Katha 5½ Dhur
2	At Vill. Phulwaria, PS-Phulwaria, Distt.-Gopalganj	Plot No. 979, Khata No. 52, Tauzi No. 3296	2 Katha 5 Dhur
3	At+Vill Vishnupura, Pargana Kuari, PS-Phulwaria, Distt.-Gopalganj	Plot No. 69M, Thana No. 862, Khata No. 54, Tauzi No. 3296	3 Katha
4	4. At Vill Selarkela, PS-Phulwaria, Distt.-Gopalganj	Plot No. 99M, Thana No. 873, Khata No. 64, Tauzi No. 3296	5 Katha 6½ Dhur

5	Mauza-Phulwaria, Panchayat-Bhagwat Parsa, Distt. Gopalganj	Khata No. 74, Survey No. 892	4 Katha 8½ Dhur
Residential Building (Includig Apartments)			
1	Mauza Hajiapur PS- Gopalganj	Khata No. 155.157. Plot No. 7 & 8(Part),9	"Land 3 Katha 2½ Dhur Building Ground Floor Built up area 3000 Sqft."
	Patna		
Agricultural Land			
1	At Mauza-Planga, PS-Phulwari Sharif, Distt- Patna	Khata No. 28, Plot No. 201, Tauzi No. 5757/18019	1 Bigha
2	At Vill Banya, PS-Phulwari Sharif, Distt.-Patna	Khata No. 581, 661, Plot No. 352 (P) 352/324	21 Katha 2 Dhur 7.75 Dhurki
Non Agricultural Land			
1	At.Vill Dhanaut PS- Danapur, Patna	Khata No. 189. Plot No. 1547	4 Katha
2	At.Vill Dhanaut PS- Danapur, Patna	Khata No. 183. Plot No. 1161 Tauzi No. 5553. Thana No. 20	8 Katha 15 Dhur
Commercial Buildings (Includig Apartments)			
1	Mauza Mazaffarpur Chitkohra PS-Gardanibagh, Distt.-Patna	Khata No.113. Survey Plot No. 1028. Tauzi No. 18215. Revenue Thana No. 17	"Land 3 Katha Building Ground Floor + 2 Floor Built up area 2000 Sqft"

Property details of Miss Raj Laxmi (Daughter)			
Patna			
Agricultural Land			
Sl.	**Locations**	**Survey No. (S)**	**Area**
1	Vill-Dhanaut,PS- Dannapur, Dist-Patna	Khata No.-183, Plot No-1161, Thana No.-20	8 Katha 15 Dhur

Property Details of Miss Dhannu (Daughter)			
Patna			
Agricultural Land			
1	Vill-Dhanaut,PS- Dannapur, Dist-Patna	Khata No.-183, Plot No.-1161, Tauzi No.-5553, Thana No.-20	6904 Sq ft.

Property details of Smt. Misha Bharti			
Patna			
Agricultural Land			
Sl	**Locations**	**Survey No.(S)**	**Area**
1	At.-Koriya, P.S.- Bihta, Distt.- Patna	Khata No.-2, Survey Plot No.-1257, 1261,1262,1263,1264,1273, 1275,1278,1279	1 Acre 85.75 Dec.
2	At.- Purushottampur, Painathi, P.S.- Bihta, Distt.- Patna	Khata No.-1023, Survey Plot No.-719	1 Acre 5 Dec.
3	At. Vill.- Bilap, P.S.- Bihta, Distt.- Patna	Khata No.-439, Survey Plot No.-172, Thana No.-3	57.5 Dec.
4	At. Vill.- Bilap, P.S.- Bihta, Distt.- Patna	Khata No.-444, Survey Plot No.-169, 139,144,146	68 Dec.
5	At. Vill.- Bilap, P.S.- Bihta, Distt.- Patna	Khata No.-438,126,511,52,126, 440,130,504 Survey Plot No.-170,184,186,195,154, 179,178	3 Acre 18.25 Dec.
Non Agricultural Land			
1	At- Mainpura,PS -Phulwari, PPS-S.K. Puri, Distt- Patna	Khata No.-421, Survey Plot No.-1310, Thana No-2	6190 Sq ft.

Property details of Shailesh Kumar (Spouse)			
Muzaffarpur			
Agricultural Land			
1	At.-Baikunthpur urph Teliya, P. S. -Kurhni, Distt.- Muzaffarpur.	Khata No.- 66, 33, 245 Kheshra No-3218, 1313, 3256	64 Dec.
2	At- Teliya, P S -Kurhni, Distt.- Muzaffarpur.	Khata No.- 160, Kheshra No-806, 808	1 Acre 32.5 Dec.
3	At- Teliya, P S -Kurhni, Distt.- Muzaffarpur.	Khata No.- 26, Kheshra No-3215	46 Dec.
4	At- Teliya, P S -Kurhni, Distt.- Muzaffarpur.	Khata No.- 151, Kheshra No-805, 809	1 Acre 93 Dec.
5	At- Teliya, P S -Kurhni, Distt.- Muzaffarpur.	Khata No.- 245, 77, Kheshra No-3162, 3163	16 Dec.
6	At- Teliya, P S -Kurhni, Distt.- Muzaffarpur.	Khata No.- 26, Kheshra No-3209	2 Dec.
Non Agricultural Land			
1	At- Teliya, P S -Kurhni, Distt.- Muzaffarpur.	Khata No.-256, Kheshra No-3205, 3214	6.5 Dec.

Patna			
Agricultural Land			
1	At & Vill-Kunjwan, P.S-Bihta,Distt-Patna	Khata No.- 2, 217 Kheshra No-285, 286, 291	2 Acre 49 Dec.
2	At & Vill-Kunjwan, P.S-Bihta,Distt-Patna	Khata No.- 2, Kheshra No-1279	67.5 Dec.

Property details of Miss Durga Bharti (Dependent 1)			
Patna			
Agricultural Land			
Sl.	**Locations**	**Survey No. (S)**	**Area**
1	At Vill- Mahuli.P S Phulwari, Distt.- Patna	Khata No.- 37, Survey Plot No.-485, Thana No.-85	72.65 Dec.
2	At- Teliya, P S -Kurhni, Distt.- Muzaffarpur.	Khata No.- 137, Kheshra No.-752	1 Acre 82 Dec.
Non Agricultural Land			
1	At-Bari Khagaul, P S -Khagaul, Distt.-Patna.	Khata No.- 8,65,92,55 Survey Plot No.-55P, 59P, 60P, 57P	3 Katha 5 Dhur

Property details of Miss Gauri Bharti (Dependent 2)			
Patna			
Agricultural Land			
1	At Vill- Mahuli.P S Phulwari, Distt.- Patna	Khata No.- 51, Survey Plot No.- 497P, Thana No.-85	68 Dec.
2	At- Teliya, P S -Kurhni, Distt.- Muzaffarpur.	Khata No.-137, Kheshra No.- 3216, 3219	1 Acre 39 Dec.
Non Agricultural Land			
1	At-Mahuli, P S -Phulwari, Distt.- Patna.	Khata No.- 40, Survey Plot No.- 495P, Thana No.-85	6.73 Dec.

□

लालू परिवार के मॉल, मिट्टी घोटाले एवं बेनामी संपत्ति का रिकॉर्ड 40 प्रेस कॉन्फ्रेंस (पी.सी.) के जरिए सिलसिलेवार खुलासा

क्रम	दिनांक	माध्यम	विषय
			अप्रैल 2017
1.	05.04.2017	पी.सी.	लालू पर जू को 90 लाख की मिट्टी बेचने के आरोप से सियासी भूचाल। बिना टेंडर गैर-कानूनी ढंग से जैविक उद्यान के लिए खरीदी गई मिट्टी, पर्यावरण और वन मंत्री को पद से बरखास्त करने की माँग की।
2.	06.04.2017		रूपसपुर में निर्माणाधीन शॉपिंग मॉल और मिट्टी बेचे जाने के आरोपों पर भाजपा आक्रामक, सर्वदलीय समिति और ई.डी. करे जाँच। लालू यादव ने जाँच की खुद माँग की है।
3.	08.04.2017	पी.सी.	लालू ने 90 नहीं, 750 करोड़ रुपयों का किया है घोटाला। अब लालू बच नहीं सकते।
4.	10.04.2017	पी.सी.	आखिरकार लालू ने कबूला कि 500 करोड़ का मॉल उनका है। 4 लाख रुपए लगाकर 500 करोड़ रुपए के मालिक बन बैठे लालू। लालू पर फिल्म बननी चाहिए।
5.	12.04.2017		लालू ने शराब फैक्टरी से भी बनाए करोड़ों। बिहटा में शराब की फैक्टरी खुलवाकर उसके मालिक ओम प्रकाश कत्याल की कंपनी की पटना शहर में स्थित करोड़ों की जमीन हथिया ली। केवल 55 हजार रुपए का निवेश करके वे करोड़ों की कंपनी के मालिक कैसे बन गए? वर्ष 2006 में ए.के. इन्फोसिस्टम्स

			प्रा.लि. कंपनी बनाई और वर्ष 2014 में तेजस्वी यादव, तेज प्रताप, चंदा और रागिनी लालू को निदेशक बनाया।
6.	14.04.2017		लालू इक्कीसवीं सदी में बिहार के सबसे बड़े जमींदार। लालू ने पार्टी के मंत्रियों, सांसदों, विधायकों और उद्यमियों से काम के बदले जमीन ली। लालू-राबड़ी के मुख्यमंत्रित्व काल में जमीन लिखवाई गई।
7.	15.04.2017	पी.सी.	तेज प्रताप यादव ने चुनाव आयोग से छिपाई औरंगाबाद की जमीन। तेज प्रताप ने वर्ष 2010 में औरंगाबाद में सात लोगों से 53.34 लाख रुपयों में कुल 45.24 डिसमिल जमीन खरीदी। जमीन को गिरवी रखकर मध्य बिहार ग्रामीण बैंक से 2.29 करोड़ रुपए का ऋण लिया।
8.	17.04.2017	पत्र	सुमो ने पर्यावरण प्राधिकार से की लालू की शिकायत। 200 करोड़ रुपए की 3 एकड़ जमीन पर लालू यादव का बिहार के सबसे बड़ा मॉल का निर्माण पिछले एक वर्ष से राज्य पर्यावरण प्रभाव आकलन प्राधिकार की अनुमति लिये बिना कराया जा रहा है, जो पर्यावरण संरक्षण अधिनियम वर्ष 1986 के प्रावधानों का उल्लंघन है।
9.	19.04.2017	पी.सी.	लालू ने बेटों की जिंदगी बरबाद कर दी है। लालू खुद 50–55 वर्ष की उम्र में जेल गए, पुत्र 25–28 वर्ष में जाएँगे। रेलमंत्री रहते लालू प्रसाद ने फर्जी कंपनियाँ बनाकर उस पर परिवार का कब्जा करवा दिया। वर्ष 2006 में ए.के. इन्फोसिस्टम्स प्रा.लि. नामक कंपनी बनाई। इसका मकराद एक ही था कि रेलमंत्री के लिए बेनामी संपत्ति खरीदना, ताकि भविष्य में जमीन सहित पूरी संपत्ति लालू परिवार को दी जा सके।
10.	20.04.2017	पी.सी.	जमीन घोटाले में शामिल कोलकाता की चौथी कंपनी फेयरग्रो होल्डिंग प्राइवेट लि. है। इस कंपनी के पास 76 लाख रुपए की जमीन है। कंपनी में तेज प्रताप,

			तेजस्वी, लालू की बेटी चंदा यादव और रागिनी लालू निदेशक हैं।
11.	21.04.2017	पत्र	सुमो ने मुख्यमंत्री को पत्र लिखकर की तेज प्रताप की शिकायत। तेज प्रताप ने चुनाव आयोग एवं बिहार सरकार से औरंगाबाद में खरीदी गई 53 लाख रुपयों की 45 डिसमिल जमीन की जानकारी जान-बूझकर छुपाई। 16 जनवरी, 2010 को जमीन का निबंधन हुआ और 12 फरवरी, 2012 को उसे गिरवी रखकर मध्य बिहार ग्रामीण बैंक, औरंगाबाद से ऋण लिया गया।
12.	22.04.2017		सुशील मोदी ने लालू प्रसाद से पूछे पाँच सवाल। सवाल—रेलमंत्री बनने के चार महीने के भीतर ही रेलवे बोर्ड से राँची व पुरी के दो होटलों को लीज पर देने का फैसला क्यों? बोर्ड के निर्णय के चार महीने के अंदर ही हर्ष कोचर ने प्रेमचंद गुप्ता की कंपनी डिलाइट मार्केटिंग को 2 एकड़ जमीन पटना में रजिस्ट्री क्यों कर दी? प्रेमचंद गुप्ता के परिवार ने कंपनी सहित जमीन लालू परिवार को क्यों सौंप दी? नोटबंदी के चार दिन बाद ही 12 नवंबर, 2016 को डिलाइट कंपनी का नाम बदलकर लारा (ला=लालू, रा=राबड़ी) प्रा.लि. क्यों कर दिया गया?
13.	23.04.2017	पी.सी.	दिल्ली में 115 करोड़ रुपयों की संपत्ति है लालू की। लालू परिवार का दिल्ली के न्यू फ्रेंड्स कॉलोनी में 800 वर्ग मीटर में फैला चार मंजिला मकान है। डिलाइट मार्केटिंग, ए.के. इन्फोसिस्टम की तर्ज पर एक और कंपनी ए.बी. एक्सपोर्ट प्राइवेट लि. है। दिल्ली की जमीन के लिए मुंबई के पाँच बड़े व्यापारियों ने वर्ष 2007-08 में ए.बी. एक्सपोर्ट को 1-1 करोड़ प्रति व्यापारी कुल 5 करोड़ रुपयों का कर्ज बिना ब्याज दे दिया।

14.	25.04.2017	पी.सी.	नहीं खरीद सकता तेजस्वी की संपत्ति। तेजस्वी ने अपनी संपत्ति 50% की छूट पर देने की बात की है। इसके बावजूद संपत्ति अरबों की है, जब कि मैं तो दो चार-लाख वाला हूँ। हाँ, 99% की छूट दें तो ले सकते हैं। जिस कंपनी में कोई कर्मचारी नहीं, कोई टर्न ओवर नहीं, आखिर उस कंपनी ने वर्ष 2007-08 में 800 वर्ग मीटर जमीन 1008, न्यू फ्रेंड्स कॉलोनी में 5 करोड़ रुपए का कर्ज लेकर क्यों खरीदी?
15.	26.04.2017	पी.सी.	केंद्र की मनमोहन सरकार में मंत्री बनाने के एवज में लालू यादव ने रघुनाथ झा से गोपालगंज का मकान बेटों के नाम से लिखवा लिया। रघुनाथ झा ने माना कि उन्होंने लालू प्रसाद के बेटों को जमीन-मकान गिफ्ट कर दिया है।
16.	27.04.2017		लालू खुद करें गिफ्ट में ली गई संपत्तियों का खुलासा। किन-किन लोगों से काम के एवज में उन्होंने जमीन, मकान और अन्य संपत्तियाँ लीं? नहीं तो भाजपा करेगी पर्दाफाश।
17.	28.04.2017	पी.सी.	लालू ने कांति सिंह से भी मंत्री बनाने के बदले ली जमीन। 95 डिसमिल बेशकीमती जमीन को 99 वर्ष के लिए लीज करा लिया। कांति सिंह को केंद्र की यू.पी.ए. सरकार में मानव संसाधन, भारी उद्योग और पर्यटन मंत्री बनवाया।
18.	29.04.2017		प्रेमचंद गुप्ता को भी राज्यसभा सांसद और मंत्री बनने की कीमत लालू यादव के परिवार को अपनी करोड़ों रुपयों की जमीन और खानदानी कंपनी देकर चुकानी पड़ी। पटना में 7 लाख वर्ग फीट में बन रहे मॉल की जमीन आखिर लालू को क्यों दिया? हरियाणा के प्रेमचंद गुप्ता में कौन सी खासियत थी कि लालू ने उन्हें पाँच बार सांसद और पाँच साल के लिए मंत्री बनाया?

मई 2017			
1.	01.05.2017		बिहार के सबसे बड़े मॉल का निर्माण पिछले एक साल से पर्यावरण नियमों का उल्लंघन कर किया जा रहा है। मीडिया में मामला उजागर होने के बाद 18 अप्रैल को सुरसंड के विधायक अबू दोजाना की कंपनी ने अनुमति के लिए राज्य पर्यावरण प्राधिकार को आवेदन दिया है, जब कि नियम उल्लंघन के बाद अब केंद्र सरकार ही अनुमति दे सकती है।
2.	06.05.2017	पी.सी.	तेज प्रताप ने पेट्रोल पंप लेने में किया फर्जीवाड़ा। फर्जी दस्तावेजों के आधार पर अफसरों की मिली-भगत से पेट्रोल पंप आवंटन करवाया है। जिस समय आवेदन दिया था, उस समय जमीन भी नहीं थी। तेज प्रताप ने तेजस्वी और लालू की जमीन का इस्तेमाल किया।
3.	12.05.2017		लालू कुनबे के खिलाफ केंद्रीय पर्यावरण एवं वन मंत्रालय के संयुक्त सचिव को ज्ञापन देकर शिकायत की कि पिछले एक साल से पर्यावरण नियमों का उल्लंघन कर हो रहा है मॉल का निर्माण।
4.	13.05.2017		लालू की बेटी-दामाद को घेरते हुए कहा कि लालू की बेटी मीसा भारती और उनके दामाद शैलेश कुमार ने मुखौटा कंपनियों के माध्यम से दिल्ली के इंदिरा गांधी अंतरराष्ट्रीय हवाई अड्डे के समीप दो फार्म हाउस खरीदे हैं, जिनका बाजार मूल्य आज लगभग 100 करोड़ रुपए है।
5.	14.05.2017	पी.सी.	लालू यादव ने चारा घोटाले के जरिए और बतौर रेलमंत्री अर्जित काले धन को ठिकाने लगाने के लिए जैन बंधुओं (वीरेंद्र जैन और सुरेंद्र जैन) का इस्तेमाल किया। जैन बंधु 8,000 करोड़ रुपयों की मनी लाउंड्रिंग के मामले में जेल में बंद हैं। इन दोनों से लालू के परिवार का सीधा संबंध है।

6.	16.05.2017	पी.सी. संवाद नीतीश कुमार	कानून का सहारा ले भाजपा। लालू यादव द्वारा अवैध जमीन खरीद मामले में भाजपा द्वारा नियमित रूप से लगाए जा रहे आरोप पर नीतीश कुमार ने कहा कि भाजपा के पास सचमुच कोई तथ्य है तो वह कानून का सहारा ले।
7.	17.05.2017	पी.सी.	लालू यादव के 22 ठिकानों पर छापे के बाद भी हमला जारी रहा। सामाजिक न्याय का ढोंग रचकर लालू प्रसाद ने गरीबों का पैसा लूटा है। राजद अध्यक्ष ने मुखौटा कंपनियों का इस्तेमाल किया। विवेक नागपाल की कंपनी के.एच.के. होल्डिंग प्रा.लि. द्वारा लालू परिवार को 50 करोड़ रुपयों से अधिक की जमीन सौंपी गई। वर्ष 1998 में मीसा भारती ने इस कंपनी को 1 लाख रुपए में खरीद लिया था।
8.	23.05.2017		लालू परिवार कहे कि बेनामी संपत्ति उनकी नहीं है। दिल्ली स्थित न्यू फ्रेंड्स कॉलोनी, बिजवासन सैनिक फार्म, औरंगाबाद व पटना में निर्माणाधीन पेट्रोल पंप की बेनामी संपत्ति उनकी नहीं है, ताकि प्रवर्तन निदेशालय इन्हें जब्त कर सके।
9.	24.05.2017	पी.सी.	जमीन में हेरा-फेरी करनेवाले होंगे बेनकाब। राजद के सांसद, विधायक ने एम.पी., विधायक गृह निर्माण को-ऑपरेटिव सोसाइटी पर कब्जा कर रखा है।
10.	25.05.2017		एम.एल.ए. हाउसिंग कमेटी को किया जाए भंग। तत्काल प्रशासक नियुक्त करें और आवंटन से संबंधित दस्तावेज को सार्वजनिक करें। 663 सदस्योंवाली को-ऑपरेटिव की वर्ष 2015 की मतदाता सूची में मेरा नाम 384 क्रमांक पर है, पर मुझे कभी भी बैठक में नहीं बुलाया गया।
11.	28.05.2017		मीसा की कंपनी को 60 लाख रुपए दिए। मीसा के सी.ए. की डायरी से पता चला कि जब लालू रेलमंत्री थे तो 8,000 करोड़ रुपए की मनी लाउंड्रिंग के आरोप में जेल में बंद वीरेंद्र जैन व सुरेंद्र जैन की

			कंपनियों के मार्फत मिशेल पैकर्स प्राइवेट लि. को बेनामी 60 लाख रुपए दिए गए।
12.	31.05.2017	पी.सी.	को-ऑपरेटिव सोसाइटी के पाँच प्लॉट्स पर लालू का कब्जा। कायदे-कानून की अनदेखी कर प्लॉट का आवंटन कराया। लालू परिवार को-ऑपरेटिव कॉलोनी में 207, 208, 209, 210 और 211 यानी कुल पाँच प्लॉट्स पर कब्जा किया है। लालू यादव ने एम.एल.सी. बनाने के लिए बादशाह प्रसाद आजाद से लाखों की जमीन मात्र 37 हजार रुपए में और सुधा श्रीवास्तव से प्लॉट नं. 151 लिखवा लिया।
जून 2017			
1.	01.06.2017		आवासीय भूखंडों से लाखों कमा रहे लालू। लालू प्रसाद जब रेलमंत्री थे, तब से उनके भूखंड संख्या 208 में गृह मंत्रालय के सीमा सुरक्षा बल का जोनल पे एंड अकाउंट ऑफिस चल रहा है। 15 साल से नियमों की धज्जियाँ उड़ाकर लाखों रुपए कमा रहे हैं।
2.	07.06.2017	पी.सी.	राबड़ी देवी ने भी ललन चौधरी नाम के एक अनजान व्यक्ति से 31 लाख रुपए की जमीन गिफ्ट में ली। ललन चौधरी ने वर्ष 2009 में यह जमीन 3.97 लाख रुपए में खरीदी थी। वह लालू की गौशाला में काम करता है।
3.	08.06.2017		पटना की कीमती जमीन अपने जानवरों को चारा खिलाने वाले ललन चौधरी के नाम लिखवा ली। बाद में जमीन की कीमत 31 लाख रुपए दिखाकर उसे राबड़ी के नाम से दान में लिखवा लिया। आखिर यह ललन चौधरी कौन है?
4.	11.06.2017	पी.सी.	ललन चौधरी देश का संभवत: ऐसा बी.पी.एल. कार्डधारी शख्स होगा, जिसने न सिर्फ 1 करोड़ रुपए की जमीन दान दी, बल्कि उसकी रजिस्ट्री के लिए स्टांप शुल्क भी खुद चुकाया। दान लेनेवाली राबड़ी देवी और उनकी बेटी हेमा यादव हैं। आयकर

			विभाग को इस बात की जाँच करनी चाहिए कि बी.पी.एल. ललन चौधरी के पास इतनी बड़ी राशि कहाँ से आई ?
5.	14.06.2017	पी.सी.	हेमा यादव को खलासी ने दान की 62 लाख रुपए की जमीन। रेलवे में खलासी पद पर कार्यरत हृदयानंद चौधरी ने भी लालू की पुत्री हेमा यादव को 62 लाख रुपए की जमीन गिफ्ट कर दी। हृदयानंद चौधरी ने 7.76 डिसमिल जमीन गिफ्ट करने के लिए 13 फरवरी, 2014 को स्टांप ड्यूटी 6 लाख 28 हजार रुपए का नकद चालान खुद जमा किया। दानकर्ता का पता '10, सर्कुलर रोड' अंकित है। हृदयानंद चौधरी के दान-पत्र में ललन चौधरी गवाह है।
6.	15.06.2017	पी.सी.	लालू कुनबे को करोड़ों की जमीन देनेवाला विधान परिषद् का कर्मी है—ललन चौधरी। लालू प्रसाद के खटाल में काम करनेवाले ललन चौधरी की नियुक्ति वर्ष 2005 में सभापति जाबिर हुसैन ने चतुर्थ श्रेणी पद पर की थी। इसी प्रकार, हृदयानंद चौधरी की नियुक्ति लालू के रेलमंत्रित्व काल में ग्रुप डी के पद पर 20 जून, 2005 को हुई थी। राबड़ी देवी और हेमा यादव ने अपनी आय कर रिटर्न में इस राशि को दरशाया है या नहीं ?
7.	17.06.2017		मीडिया पर राज्य सरकार लगा रही पाबंदी। राबड़ी-हेमा को करोड़ों की संपत्ति देनेवाले वि.प. कर्मी ललन चौधरी को नीतीश कुमार के इशारे पर लालू यादव छुपाकर रखे रहे। अब मीडिया ने उसे खोजकर निकाला है तो सरकार खीज उतार रही है।
8.	18.06.2017		काले धन और बेनामी संपत्ति के खिलाफ अंबार खड़ा करनेवाले मंत्रियों पर काररवाई क्यों नहीं करते ? मुख्यमंत्री बताएँ भ्रष्टाचार पर जीरो टॉलरेंस की नीति का क्या हुआ ? मुख्यमंत्री काररवाई से बचते हैं और चाहते हैं कि केंद्र सरकार काररवाई करे, ताकि साँप भी मर जाए और लाठी भी न टूटे।

9.	21.06.2017	पी.सी.	पटना में राबड़ी देवी के 18 फ्लैट्स हैं। पटना शहर में 18,600 वर्ग फीट में बने कॉम्प्लेक्स में राबड़ी देवी के 18 फ्लैट्स हैं, जिनकी कीमत 20 करोड़ रुपए है। दानापुर और शेखपुरा मौजा में दो जमीन तीन ऐसे लोगों से लिखवाई, जिनके परिवार को रेलवे में नौकरी दी गई। वर्ष 2011 में श्रेया कंस्ट्रक्शन के अमरेंद्र कुमार सिन्हा से कॉम्प्लेक्स बनाने के लिए एग्रीमेंट किया।
10.	22.06.2017	पी.सी.	आयकर विभाग ने तेजस्वी/तेज प्रताप की 175 करोड़ रुपए की 14 बेनामी संपत्ति को जब्त करने का आदेश दिया है, इसलिए मुख्यमंत्री भ्रष्टाचार में लिप्त मंत्री को बरखास्त करें।
11.	28.06.2017	पी.सी.	लालू की कोलकाता में भी संपत्ति। लालू प्रसाद द्वारा बेनामी कंपनी फेयरग्रो प्राइवेट लि. के माध्यम से 76 लाख रुपए में कोलकाता में एक मकान खरीदने और बाद में कंपनी के डायरेक्टर को हटाकर कंपनी को हड़पने का मामला सामने आया। इसकी कीमत 10 करोड़ रुपए है। सभी खोखा कंपनियों से बेनामी संपत्ति हासिल करने का काम। कोलकाता के के.पी. सरागवी और
			ए.के. महेश्वरी ने सन् 1991 में 35 लाख रुपए में फेयरग्रो प्राइवेट लि. कंपनी 130/1, बाकुल बाग रोड, थाना–भवानीपुर, कोलकाता के पते पर स्थापित की थी।
जुलाई 2017			
1.	05.07.2018	पी.सी.	44 महीने की उम्र में 13 एकड़ जमीन के मालिक थे तेज प्रताप। वर्ष 1993 में पूर्व मंत्री बृज बिहारी प्रसाद की पत्नी रमा देवी ने तेज प्रताप को 13 एकड़ 12 डिसमिल जमीन दान की। जब जमीन दान में दी गई, उस समय तेज प्रताप 3 वर्ष 8 माह के ही थे। जमीन मुजफ्फरपुर के किशुनगंज थाना कुढ़नी में है।

2.	06.07.2018	पी.सी.	2,000 करोड़ रुपए का मालिक बना लालू परिवार। लालू परिवार ने बारह वर्षों में बिना किसी व्यापार, उद्योग या ठेकेदारी किए विभिन्न शहरों में 2,000 करोड़ रुपयों से अधिक की 125 से ज्यादा संपत्तियाँ अर्जित कीं। रेलमंत्री रहते बड़े-बड़े ठेके और लीज तथा नौकरियाँ देकर अकूत संपत्ति अर्जित की। भ्रष्टाचार और मुखौटा कंपनियों के माध्यम से कीमती जमीन खरीदकर लालू के परिवार ने संपत्ति के मामले में हथुआ और दरभंगा महाराज को भी पीछे छोड़ दिया।
3.	07.07.2018	पी.सी.	कोर्ट में भी कहूँगा—लालू है भ्रष्टाचारी। भ्रष्टाचारी को भ्रष्टाचारी कहने में कोई संकोच नहीं है। मुकदमों से मैं नहीं डरता हूँ। लालू में हिम्मत है तो गिफ्ट में मिली सभी जमीनें वापस करें।
4.	08.07.2018	पी.सी.	लालू आवास पर सी.बी.आई. की छापेमारी के बाद तेजस्वी यादव पर इस्तीफे का दबाव बनाया। तेजस्वी पर भ्रष्टाचार का मुकदमा दर्ज है, ऐसे में नैतिकता के नाते उन्हें इस्तीफा देना चाहिए।
5.	09.07.2018		अगर तेजस्वी में हिम्मत है तो सी.बी.आई. के आरोपों का बिंदुवार जवाब दें। लालू ने भी चारा घोटाला के समय काफी बयानबाजी की, पर इस्तीफा देना ही पड़ा था।
6.	10.07.2018		चारा और लारा घोटाले से बिहार बदनाम हुआ। राजद विधायक से अपील है कि लालू+राबड़ी पर 1,000 करोड़ की बेनामी संपत्ति के मामले में आरोपित तेजस्वी से इस्तीफा दिलवाने और राजद के वरिष्ठ सदस्य जैसे सिद्दीकी जी या ललित यादव को उनकी जगह दिलवाए। लालू जब जेल गए थे तो कहा था कि खून की नदी बह जाएगी। पर एक पत्ता तक नहीं हिला था।

7.	12.07.2018		नीतीश कुमार द्वारा तेजस्वी को सी.बी.आई. छापे और भ्रष्टाचार के मामले में दी गई नसीहत को भाजपा ने सराहा। अब गेंद तेजस्वी के पाले में है।
8.	13.07.2018		नाबालिग कहकर अपराधों पर परदा नहीं डाल सकते तेजस्वी। सी.बी.आई. की एफ.आई.आर. के आरोपी तेजस्वी पर बेनामी संपत्ति हासिल करने का आरोप तब का है, जब वह निमुछिया नहीं, बल्कि दाढ़ी-मूँछवाले, यानी बालिग हो चुके थे।
9.	14.07.2018		तेजस्वी यादव को भाजपा नहीं, बल्कि लालू ने अपने भ्रष्टाचार में साझीदार बनाकर फँसा दिया।
10.	15.07.2018		तेजस्वी यादव के इस्तीफे को लेकर जदयू और राजद के घमासान के बीच भाजपा ने भ्रष्टाचार पर मुख्यमंत्री नीतीश की जमकर तारीफ की। भ्रष्टाचार पर नीतीश का स्टैंड हमेशा ही साफ रहा है। नीतीश कुमार ने भ्रष्टाचार से कभी भी समझौता नहीं किया है।
11.	16.07.2018		तेजस्वी को अविलंब बरखास्त करें नीतीश कुमार। राजद, लालू और तेजस्वी ने जदयू की सभी तीन
			शर्तों को ठुकरा साफ कर दिया है कि न तो तेजस्वी इस्तीफा देंगे, न लालू प्रसाद अपनी बेनामी संपत्ति का खुलासा करेंगे और न ही सी.बी.आई., ई.डी. और आय कर विभाग द्वारा लगाए गए आरोपों का बिंदुवार तथ्यात्मक जवाब देंगे।
12.	19.07.2018		मूँछ के बाद भी बनाई बेनामी संपत्ति। तेजस्वी 26 वर्ष की उम्र में 26 संपत्तियों के मालिक बने, जिसमें से 13 संपत्तियों के मालिक नाबालिग रहते बने थे, जबकि 13 संपत्तियों के मालिक बालिग होने के बाद बने। 24 वर्ष के थे, तभी डिलाइट मार्केटिंग के शेयर पूरी तरह से ट्रांसफर किए गए। 16 वर्ष के थे तो कांति सिंह और रघुनाथ झा की करोड़ों की जमीन और मकान दान में ले लिये।

13.	23.07.2018		तेजस्वी यादव के मुद्दे पर सदन नहीं चलने देगी भाजपा। नीतीश कुमार ने बिंदुवार जवाब माँगा था, पर राजद ने चुप्पी साध ली है।
14.	25.07.2018		हवाला कांड में आरोप लगने मात्र पर इस्तीफा देनेवाले शरद यादव आज गठबंधन बचाने की आड़ में तेजस्वी यादव के भ्रष्टाचार का समर्थन कर रहे हैं। जनादेश किसी तरह से गठबंधन चलाने के लिए नहीं, बल्कि भ्रष्टाचार और अपराध पर प्रभावी अंकुश लगाने को मिला है।
15.	28.07.2018		लालू ने पुत्र-मोह में गँवा दी सूबे की सत्ता।

अगस्त 2017 से मई 2018 तक की पी.सी.

1.	07.08.2017	पी.सी.	बालू माफियाओं ने खरीदे राबड़ी के 3 फ्लैट्स।
2.	18.08.2017	पी.सी.	एक और बालू माफिया ने खरीदे राबड़ी के 5 फ्लैट्स।
3.	20.08.2017	पी.सी.	बिहार लोक सेवा आयोग का चेयरमैन एवं राज्यपाल कोटे से एम.एल.सी. बनाने के बदले
			पटना में करोड़ों की जमीन को लालू परिवार ने हथियाया।
4.	30.08.2017	पी.सी.	राज्यपाल कोटे से पार्षद बनाने के एवज में मो. शमीम और सोफिया तबस्सुम से वसीयत कराया
5.	06.09.2017	पी.सी.	तेजस्वी और 4 संपत्तियों के मालिक बने (28 साल की उम्र में 30 संपत्तियों के मालिक बने तेजस्वी)। मो. शमीम के बाद कुमार राकेश रंजन से भी जमीन वसीयत करवा ली।
6.	19.09.2017	पी.सी.	750 करोड़ रुपए के 15 मंजिला बिहार के सबसे बड़े मॉल का निर्माण बिना नक्शा पास कराए प्रारंभ किया गया था।
7.	10.10.2017	पी.सी.	दान-वसीयत की कड़ी में अब सुभाष चंद्र चौधरी-मीसा भारती को किया 4 कट्ठा 11 धुर जमीन दान।

8.	17.10.2017	पी.सी.	11वीं दानकर्ता श्रीमती चंद्रकांता देवी ने लालू प्रसाद की बड़ी बेटी मीसा भारती को 318 डिसमिल जमीन दान में दी।
9.	24.10.2017	पी.सी.	मिट्टी घोटाले की जाँच निगरानी से कराने का निर्णय।
10.	07.11.2017	पी.सी.	शराब माफिया से लाभ लेते रहे तेजस्वी।
11.	21.11.2017	पी.सी.	आवामी को-ऑपरेटिव बैंक लालू की दुधारू गाय।
12.	28.04.2018	पी.सी.	एक और मुखौटा कंपनी के माध्यम से करोड़ों की संपत्ति के मालिक बने तेजस्वी यादव।
13.	30.04.2018	पी.सी.	टाटा स्टील की संपत्ति के भी मालिक तेजस्वी।
14.	02.05.2018	पी.सी.	टिस्को (TISCO)की संपत्ति तेजस्वी को देने के लिए सहारा समूह ने भुगतान किया।

□□□

www.ingramcontent.com/pod-product-compliance
Lightning Source LLC
LaVergne TN
LVHW040757260325
806810LV00009B/166/J